BONESPURS

Short Stories and Flash Fiction

By

Ronald T Ray

Isbn # 978-1-312-56252-3

Front cover illustration by Ronald Ray
Back cover illustration by LuChristie Waites

'A Brief Dialogue with the Dead' and 'Mannequin' were co-written
with LuChristie Waites

This is a work of fiction. Names, characters, places, events and
incidents are either products of the author's imagination or used in a
fictitious manner. Any resemblance to actual persons, living or dead, or
actual events is purely coincidental.

CONTENTS

Wide-Eyed

Look here, Wonderbread, this ain't no muh-fuckin' shoe sale. This is gun-in-your-face-pop-a-cap-in-your-ass for real. These people been in my head too long, they all be talkin' at the same time. Ripsnark is the loudest, yellin' above all the others just that one word, over and over… "Kill! Kill! Kill!"

I don't know how much more I can stand. It's too damn crowded in here, too close, sweat drips from one to the other. Some don't even speak English. They just be jabberin' away like I know what they want. One even talks like you, Wonderbread, all proper and pronounciated. Maybe he is you. He tries to keep it all together, keep the riff-raff in check. They stopped listening to him, though, and I'm scared, man.

I dreamt last night I was out in the ocean, so far I couldn't see land. It was scary, but kinda nice for a while. So quiet and peaceful… Then I was back in the apartment, and I felt like a volcano about to blow. That's when I called you. So can you fix me, Wonderbread? Gimme some pills, or shots, somthin' to kill the rats runnin' 'round my head? If you can't, you know you'll be the first to go. And don't be callin' no po-lice. We'll both be gone before they get here.

Harvey & June

Harvey ate a bug. June just stared at him, so he ate another.

"You're disgusting." she monotoned.

"Thank you." he replied, just as flatly.

Harvey: "I want a new hat. Not really a new one, though. Actually, what I want is a battered old top hat. Wouldn't that be cool?"

June: "Yeah, pretty cool. I want a pope hat."

Harvey: "You can't be pope, you're a girl."

June: "I don't want to be pope, I just want the hat. But I could be pope.

Harvey: "What's for dinner?"

June: "You just had yours. I'm having Chinese."

Harvey: "I want Burrito Loco."

June: "You're halfway there."

Harvey: "Thank you."

June: "No, thank *you*."

Harvey: "No, thank YOU!"

June: "OK, we're both thanked. Give me a cigarette."

Harvey: "You can't have one, your heart will explode."

June: "I want one anyway."

Harvey: "OK."

June: (lights up and immediately explodes all over the room.)

Harvey. "Damn."

Diner

The diner was old, even then. Shafts of light shone through the picture-window blinds over the faded red booths. Two waitresses worked there; one red-haired with too much rouge, the other grey-haired with glasses. They both wore white uniforms, dresses. Women didn't wear pants much, back then. The cook was tattooed and also wore white. He looked as much like a sailor as a cook.

Tall menus were sandwiched between napkin holders and salt & pepper shakers on the sides of the tables by the window. There were no booths on the other side, just a counter with stools.

Coca-Cola, iced tea, coffee. Burgers and fries with a real bottle of ketchup on the table. Ham and eggs anytime, pork chops, ribs. The customers were mostly men; truckers, travelling salesmen, men with no wives to cook for them. Occasionally a family, in from shopping the dusty shops of Main Street.

Inside the diner, Sharon wrung her gnarled hands and worried, worried about the dust, the dreams, the disease.

The bell above the door tinkled and broke her reverie. The Sparkling Man was here again. Light rushed to fill the shadowed corners. Sharon was suddenly young again, her hands smooth, her back straight.

The aged jukebox began whispering a Duke Ellington tune. The light had become so bright now that she could only see a flood of angel dust through the door frame.

The diner was gone. The sparkling Man was gone. Nothing but white light, lazy dust, and the open door.

Sharon was afraid to blink, afraid that if she did the world would come back. "I will not blink," she thought. Not this time. Wide-eyed, she walked resolutely towards the door.

A Funeral

The girls wore death masks and long white robes trimmed in gold. The masks were white, painted with designs and gold sparkles. They carried a white coffin, bent not with its weight but with their grief. Down to the river, beneath the willows, to a hole dug in the soft earth. That's where they buried their sister that sorrowful day in June. That day that wanted to rain, but didn't; not until she was safe in the ground.

Four elements, four seasons, but now only seven sisters. The rain began, and lasted seven days. Everyone in the land had vivid, disturbing dreams. It drove some of the more fragile insane; it affected the work of all. Things taken for granted, like the seasons coming in order, became strange and unpredictable. All because of an event they knew nothing of, a funeral they never attended.

It went on for seven years, until the birth of a new sister. Not a mortal soul knew why.

Charlie

Charlie couldn't dance anymore. His legs went bad, arthritis in the knees. It was a real tragedy, because Charlie always enjoyed the attention his dancing brought. It was the one thing that he could do well, and now it was gone. He'd never been much of a singer, and it was rather pitiful to hear him trying now, trying anything to grab the spotlight just a little longer. Charlie could feel death, and it wasn't far away. He couldn't speak about it to anyone but me, because it wasn't something you went around telling people. But he knew it was near, he told me. I was his confidant. Why, I don't know. He just took a liking to me for some reason. I was as young as you are when I first met him, when I was sneaking into bars and badgering people for drinks. Charlie always bought me one.

Charlie hobbled off the stage with his cane to a smattering of applause, mostly sympathetic. I guess some were drunk enough to think they'd just heard Sinatra. Mostly sympathetic, though. We sat at a table and had a couple before I drove him home to Amberwood, the old folks' home. He'd been there for almost a year now, and if anyone could tell when death was around it was him. Death was a frequent visitor there, everyone knew him. Did you know death had a name? I never did, until Charlie told me. He said his name was Mr. Marston, and that he wasn't spooky at all. In fact, Charlie said, he was a rather kindly gent in a pin-stripe suit. A lot of the residents of Amberwood would actually brighten up when he came in, hoping he'd come for them this time. Charlie wasn't in any big hurry, but he'd lost his shine when his legs went bad. I don't think he cared much one way or the other.

I woke up this morning to the smell of stale beer and cigarette smoke. I wished for the thousandth time that just once it would be coffee and bacon frying. It never was, though. I made a cold bologna sandwich, ate it standing over the sink, and crawled back into bed. I dozed off and on the rest of the day, with the TV on for company. I don't know why I never found a good woman, one who'd straighten me up and make me into something. I just never did, and I was pretty used to it now. There was one though, especially, that I still think about now and then. But that was long ago, and neither here nor there. It was time to pick up Charlie, and I was already tasting the beer I'd soon have.

When I pulled up in the parking lot, I saw Charlie walking out the door beside a man in a pin-stripe suit. He wasn't using his cane, he was walking just fine. I couldn't move; I just sat there gawking. Even from that distance, I could see the twinkle in Charlie's eye as he danced a few steps along the way. Before I could think to move, they'd faded into the darkness towards the park. I was sad that I wouldn't see Charlie again, but happy that his legs were all right now. I wished for a minute that I'd chased after them, to see if I could go too. But I knew that wasn't how it worked. I drove to the bar, and told the manager Charlie wouldn't be coming in anymore. Then I bought the house a round with the rent money. What the hell.

Has-Been

Tony Vegas was a crooner in a world of screamers. He wore sharkskin suits while everyone around him wore tie-dye tee shirts and jeans. Tony was past his prime, and he knew it. The cigarettes and whiskey had given his voice an unwanted edge. It was becoming hard for him to get jobs even in small clubs now. People didn't want to hear it anymore. Tony remembered Charlie, dying in a nursing home. He wasn't much older than he was now. He tossed back a shot of bourbon and lit a cigarette. He needed a gimmick. He could start wearing jeans and playing guitar to his same old songs; but these kids now, they knew a faker. Maybe a broad to do duets with? She'd have to have a good deal of popularity on her own, though. He couldn't think of anyone like that who'd want to sing with him. Especially with his history regarding women. Maybe more comedy in his act? He'd always had a good rapport with his audience, maybe a little more comedic patter between songs? "Who're you kidding?" he thought. He looked down from his tenth-floor suite at the city below and wondered what would happen if he jumped. Would it kill him, or just fuck him up and make things worse. Besides, his Catholic upbringing pretty much nixed that option. He wasn't religious, but he wasn't crazy, either. Well, he might not have a show lined up for next week, but he had one tonight. He took another drink and called a cab.

Chopping Wood

The dreams; every night they played in the theatre of my mind, vivid, colorful, sick. Dismembered limbs fell from spring blue skies, dark blood spattering the bright green leaves of the trees and plants. Faces with mouths screaming, fingers pointing. Every morning, my mind was fogged, confused, a little moreso than the previous morning. The dreams. They were becoming more colorful than reality. The world I walked through in a waking state (more or less, anyway; tired, tired, always so tired, and so sleepy...) the "real world" gradually became dark, drained of color, hazy, like an old film...

I was walking through a misty forest, a familiar place from my childhood. Sunlight reached down through the tops of the foliage like fingers. The ground was carpeted in layer upon layer of dead, rotting leaves, and the slightest sound echoed through the heavy air in a strange, solid sounding way. There wasn't much sound: the leaves beneath my feet were moist, almost noiseless. The occasional cry of a bird or owl pierced the air and stopped, as though even the inhabitants of the forest were prone to whisper rather than cry. And then I heard it. From far away, the chopping sound that I remembered. How many years had it been, but still that dreadful sound! A slow, slightly uneven rhythm... impossible to tell where it originated, from deep within the shadows, somewhere...

I began to tremble. I could no longer tell if I was awake or in a dream. What had been was the same as what was now. I didn't want to move, but my feet kept taking me forward. I *must* be in a dream; I couldn't control my own actions. I knew that there was a house, unpainted, derelict, an awful place, that I'd be coming upon soon. I don't want to go there, help me, why can't I turn around and run?! The chopping sound was growing louder. I had no will of my own. "Our Father, who art in heaven, hallowed be thy name..." I began repeating mindlessly under my breath. And then, as the house came into view through the mist, "This is not real. I'm only dreaming. This is not real. I'm only dreaming..."

I saw him as he saw me. Standing out by the building, a little shed, ax in hand. In the first few seconds, it was only a man taking a break from cutting cord wood. Then he was covered in blood, soaked through his clothes, matted through his hair. The cord wood stacked against the shed was pale and spattered with blood. His eyes were mad, staring, but they were *my* eyes. MY eyes.

It's been a long time. I don't know how long, time doesn't seem to exist here in the same way that it does elsewhere. I go into town sometimes, but only at night. I bring back my wood and I chop and stack it. Sometimes, I see a ghost, standing and staring at me, but I'm not scared. I feel as though I know him.

Death of a Plastic Salesman

"Jesus!" he said. Then again. "JESUS!" It sounded as though he was calling for him. Did he think that if he yelled loud enough, Jesus would amble in and ask him what he wanted? This plastic man in a green suit with orange pinstripes. His mouth was constantly opening into a gaping toothy grin, but his eyes never smiled. The eyes calculated, taking in information, deciding with computer-like speed what to use and how best to use it, what to ignore, and what to file away for future reference. He was hollow. I could see the wall behind him, but evidently I was the only one. The crowd's faces looked up at him in rapture, in an almost sexual frenzy. They clapped, they threw up their arms, they shouted out "Praise the Lord!"

I lost interest and watched the dust particles dancing in a ray of sunlight from the window, warm and hazy, like a memory not quite remembered. I drifted away to the Place, where the noise and confusion becomes a soft murmur in the background. I walked through fields spotted with daisies, fluffy white clouds floating by overhead... bodies need rest. I don't know how long I stayed, time doesn't matter there. I heard a bird scream, and I knew that my time was up. Suddenly everything began to turn crimson. Red drops on daisies. Sky flooded with raging red. I couldn't breathe. Eyes squeezed shut. Pulse pounded brain. No. No. NO. Not again. I knew what I would see when I opened my eyes, but I had to anyway. I had to.

Green suit soaked red white office walls spattered papers scattered deranged is what they said but the hollow man was down and out and something was not all bad about the picture.

It was dark outside. I slipped out a back door unnoticed, if there was anyone there to notice. I didn't really care.

Later I remembered how hard the plastic man's hair had been, like a hat. I don't know why I thought of that. Maybe because the pressure in my own head was gone, and I didn't have to think about using a drill on it anymore. Not for a while.

The Little Men in William's Head

William fumbled through the cabinet for his pain pills. He knew they were there; they'd been there yesterday, hadn't they? He knew damn well he hadn't imagined it. He pulled up a chair and stood on it so that he could see all the way back into the cabinet. Some old cigars he'd forgotten about, but no pills.

Cursing under his breath, he put the chair back and went to the bedroom to lie down. The shades and curtains were drawn against the July light. He wished that he'd gotten a cool cloth to put on his head, but he wasn't getting back up for anything now. The pain was behind his eyes, excruciating. At least it was quiet. The white noise of the air conditioning unit lulled him into a troubled sleep.

He dreamed of little men inside his head doing construction work. Their hammers and saws pounded and stabbed. He wondered what they were building in there; a monument to his extreme stupidity? He couldn't help the things he did when these migraines happened. Being uncivil to his neighbors was not in his nature, but everything went to hell when he was in such pain. Should he be held responsible for his actions when he had so little control over them?

He'd almost made Jenna cry, when all she wanted was help unscrewing the lid from a jar. Right now, he hated himself and the world, and more than anything those busy little men.

The phone rang. It sounded like voices screaming from hell. He covered his ears and waited for it to stop. The tinnitus kicked in then, joining the noise in his head with the sounds of cicadas and the humming of electricity through wires. What the fuck could have happened to his pills? If he survived this attack, that would be his first order of business. Find the damned pills.

Eventually it all subsided, and he slept away the afternoon.

When he awoke, it was seven o'clock; still light outside, but not the glaring midday sun that he despised. He found the pills exactly where he'd looked before. Shaking his head in disbelief, he moved them to the nightstand by his bed. He checked his messages. His mother had called. He'd call her back tomorrow, he thought. He still wasn't in the mood to carry on a conversation with anyone. William (Doobie to his oldest friends) turned on the television, keeping the sound down low. He had a book that hadn't been read yet, but he didn't want to risk doing anything that might make his pain return. He lit one of the old cigars and watched cartoons. There was a baseball game on, but he didn't feel like hearing the noise. He wished Chrissie were here. She'd have had a cup of coffee ready for him when he got up, maybe a sandwich. He was too lazy to get up and get either for himself.

Chrissie was visiting her family in Arizona for a couple of weeks. The apartment always felt so empty when she was gone, even though neighbors dropped by occasionally. He'd have to apologize to Jenna. But not now. Tomorrow, things would be better. Tonight, he'd have a few beers and watch Adult Swim on the cartoon network. He remembered the nights when he would've been smoking weed instead of a cigar. He didn't really miss it.

There was a knock on the door. Harry.

"Hey, don't you want to come outside with us? We're barbecuing."

"No thanks, Harry, I'm just getting over a migraine. Tell everyone I said hi, though."

"Ok, will do. Hope you feel better soon."

"I'm sure I'll be all right by tomorrow. Thanks."

William fell asleep on the sofa around four AM watching 'Aqua Team Hunger Force.' He dreamed of the little men building in his head. Even though only the framework was done, he could see what it was; a spaceship! He could even hear talking; something about evacuation plans, and when they'd be ready to go.

The dream stayed with him when he awoke late the next morning. He must have gotten up and went to bed at some point, but he didn't remember it. Things had been slipping his mind lately. He was having problems with his memory, remembering numbers and names. He really should tell the doctor next time he saw him, he thought. At fifty-six, he knew that early Alzheimer's was possible. It definitely wasn't unheard of. The little men were taking up too much room in his mind, maybe. He wished that he could clear the little bastards out... maybe it would give him more memory space.

He ate a bologna sandwich for breakfast and called Chrissie, then his mom. All was well with both of them. The rest of the day lay open before him. What would he do to fill it? He went next door and apologized to Jenna, telling her about the migraine. Things were smoothed over there. He wished that he had someone to tell about the strange dreams, but he wasn't close enough to anyone to be talking like a nutcase. He could feel them there in the back of his mind all the time now.

The day passed uneventfully. He did go outside for a while and stand around smoking and talking with some of the other men from the building. He thought about riding his bike to get a little exercise, but never got around to it. He was pretty happy just to be feeling fairly well. He began reading 'Shards' by William Barker. After the first few pages, he found it harder and harder to concentrate. The little men were pounding away behind his eyes, and didn't seem to like the disturbance. He took a pain pill right away, just in case. As the sky began its slow descent into darkness, he realized that he'd forgotten to eat since the morning's sandwich. He called out for a small pizza; he forgot to tip the delivery guy.

William's problems were getting worse. It wasn't just names and numbers that he was forgetting now. Sometimes he couldn't find the right word to say what he meant. Sometimes a word that he'd known all of his life seemed strange and alien; he couldn't understand its meaning. He gave up trying to read and talked to no one any more than he had to. "Am I becoming a moron?" he thought.

Meanwhile, he was monitoring the construction progress in his dreams. The migraines were coming every two days or so, but he managed to keep up with his pills. They helped, but didn't keep him from dreaming about Them, even when he was only dozing. The ship was nearing completion. Would he be normal again once they left? Who were they?

The days and nights ran together, long and lonely. Chrissie would be back in two days, he was glad of that. Maybe he could broach the subject with her. He hadn't told her about any of these problems, he wanted her to enjoy her vacation.

He stopped answering the phone or the door. It was too hard to form words, too hard to understand the words of others. He forgot to eat or bathe. All he did was watch the little men as they made the last preparations for take-off. He could see them now even when awake; all he had to do was close his eyes.

When Chrissie called from the airport and didn't get an answer, she knew that something was wrong. Taking a taxi home, she unlocked the door to find William sitting on the sofa with the Cartoon Network on TV. He was staring at the television, but not seeing it. Drool was running down his half-open mouth, and he had soiled himself. The little men were gone, and so was William.

Unintentional

Adrian Casket and Vera Mulch walked down to the Bluelight Lounge. It was a cool summer's eve in Rockford; the day was settling down for a nap, the stars were waking up. They could hear the music long before they reached their destination. "Back in the Saddle" by Aerosmith. By the time they walked in, it had changed to "Stairway to Heaven". A sole couple on the dance floor were holding each other up through the epic tune. The bar was already half-full of people drinking and shouting at each other over the music. The pool table was being used, as was the dart board. In the back room there were vintage games, pinball, Pac-man, Frogger, Foosball. Adrian and Vera never went into the back; neither had ever cared much for gaming. They went to the bar and ordered two rum-and-cokes and settled into a corner table. Now the Talking Heads were burning down the house, and several couples hit the dance floor. Adrian and Vera drank in silence. Adrian thought it was a damned shame that you couldn't smoke in the bars anymore; the sweet taste of the rum-and-coke begged for a cigarette chaser. After half a glass, he excused himself to go outside for a smoke.

He'd only taken a few long drags when he heard a popping sound from inside, like firecrackers. Suddenly people were running out of the front door, some with dark stains on their clothing. "Damn, not again!" he thought. He awoke in the double bed with the empty space beside him. Four fucking years, and he was still having the dream. It was always exactly the same, beginning to end. He looked at the clock. Four AM. He got up, peed, splashed some water on his face, and put the coffee on.

"Another great day ahead", he thought. By five he was riding his bike down to the cemetery. He'd done it every day for over four years, placing a single rose on her grave. He didn't know how much longer he'd do it, but for now he couldn't stop himself. He knew that the overwhelming guilt he felt for not being there with her was wrong; being inside wouldn't have made any difference, except for the fact that he might not be here now either. Still, what the brain knows is not always what the heart feels. He had a cold slice of leftover pizza for breakfast, then got his other daily duty out of the way; looking at the pills that he'd hoarded, wondering if today would be the day. No, not today. Soon, maybe, but not today. He sat down at his computer and tried to write, but this is what came out. He didn't mean to write this

A Eulogy of Sorts

Every family has that uncle. You know, the one whose presence at a family gathering always causes tension until everyone's sure he's back on his medication. The one who's usually prefaced by a "poor," as in "Poor Uncle Frank." Yeah, that one.

Bobby: "Me 'n' Dad went to Uncle Frank's last summer. His house was old 'n' dirty 'n' he was in his underwear." (giggles)

Mother 1: "Ssssh!"

Sarah: (whispering) "Mama always made us hug him and he smelled funny!"

Bobby: "My mom said we didn't have to hug him, but Jesus would love us more if we did."

Sarah: (suppressed chuckling)

Mother 2: "Ssssh!"

Father 2: "They're only speaking their minds, for chrissake. Poor guy *was* a raving lunatic. His death is a blessing in disguise, I tell you."

Mother 2: "Don't you speak like that in the house of God! He was my brother! He did the best he could with the cards life dealt him."

Father 2: "Oh, come on! He spent his government check on beer and ammunition every month and lived on handouts from the rest of us."

Mother 2: "You *know* that he couldn't help it! He was a decent man, he just had his demons."

Father 1: "Did you know he used to sit on the porch in the dark all night and shoot anything that moved? It's a damned wonder he wasn't locked away."

Mother 1: "Shut up, Harold! Like *you've* never been locked up?"

Father 1: (looking very dark) "That's different and you know it!"

Mother 2: "It's sad so few of the family showed up. He didn't have many friends."

Mother 1: "Yes, it is. But you know, people have their lives. John missed a day's pay to be here, and not everyone can afford that."

Mother 2: "Still...."

Mother 1: "Yes, I know. It *is* a shame."

Sarah: "Mama, why does God make broke people like Uncle Frank? Why don't he fix them?"

Mother 2: "It's all part of His Great Plan. We don't know why God does things; we just have to trust Him."

Father 2: (amused) "Some great plan!"

Mother 2: (glares silently)

Bobby: "Is it over yet? I'm hungry!"

Mother 1: "Yes, it's over now."

Last Conversation with Penelope

"You're killing yourself, don't you care?"

"I said bring me another beer."

"Dammit, John, if you don't care about yourself, at least try for me!"

"Fuck it, I'll get it myself."

"You know how much I love you. It's killing me to see you slowly destroy yourself."

"Would you rather I did it more quickly?"

"I hate you."

"I thought you just said that you loved me."

"I can't talk to you when you're like this. I'm going to bed."

"Good idea. I'll be along in a little while. I just need to do a little writing."

"How can you write when you can barely see?"

"Goodnight, sweetheart, it's time to go…"

(Bedroom door slams shut.)

("Don't Fear the Reaper" begins to play on the stereo.)

The Last Word

"You always have to get in the last word."

"What the hell do you mean? I rarely get a chance to get in a word at all!"

"You know that's not true, Daniel Roberts!"

"Well here's my last word for tonight…"

He pretended to snore. Janie turned her back to him and turned out the lamp.

As his snoring became real, she lay there in the darkness thinking. Was this what married life was supposed to be about? Why did they constantly argue and bicker, especially over things that weren't important to either of them. This was all wrong; nothing like the romantic notions she'd had two years ago when they were married. Daniel farted loudly in his sleep. As she drifted off to sleep herself, she was thinking of the phrase "Don't go away angry… just go away."

In her dream, she was standing at a crossroads in the moonlight. A dark figure approached her. Try as she might, she couldn't see his face. He spoke to her.

"I can fix your problems, Janie. I can make everything be as wonderful as you'd imagined."

"Who are you? And what makes you think you can help me?"

"My name is not important. I am known by many names. I have known you since you were born. I know your wishes and desires. Remember Tom Riley in seventh grade? What a crush you had on him. How you cried when he rejected you."

"How could you possibly know that?"

"I know a lot of things, Janie. I know how you dreamed of your wedding day, and how beautiful you wanted it to be. You didn't get to wear a white dress, did you? You were married in a civil service in an office. You went out for pizza and beer afterwards instead of a champagne reception."

"What's done is done. How could you possibly change things now? Just who are you?"

"I'll give you a little clue. My favorite song is 'Sympathy for the Devil.' So have a little courtesy and respect, please."

"Jesus Christ!"

"Jesus has nothing to do with it. I can bring you happiness. All Jesus ever did was bring you Daniel."

"Even if you can do what you say, you'll be wanting my soul in return. I know the deal. I've read enough books, seen enough movies."

"You've read and seen lies, my dear. It's I who am the good guy. Your god has let the world fester in violence, war, disease, famine. I do what little I can to help people like you. Of course, if you don't want my help, there are plenty of others waiting who will be glad to receive it."
He turned as if to leave.

"No, wait. Tell me exactly how you would help me?"

"You'll have to trust me on that. All you have to do is ask. There are no contracts to be signed in blood, none of that ridiculous claptrap that you've heard of. Just tell me you want my help."

"God help me, I do. My life is miserable. I want to start again, fresh. I want to be happy."

"And so it shall be. You can go back to sleep now. I'll take care of everything."

Janie woke up in her dorm room at UNC. Her roommate Kathy was already up.

"Better hurry, Janie, you'll be late for class."

"I had the longest, strangest dream! I dreamed that I'd dropped out of school to marry Daniel Roberts! What a bum he turned out to be!"

19

Kathy laughed.

"I'll slap you silly if you ever do something that stupid."

"There was something else about the dream... something really weird... but I can't remember it now."

"Maybe you'll remember it later. Get dressed! It's time for Professor Wonderful!"

"Oh, the naughty things I could do with that man!"

Laughing, they gathered their books and headed off to class.

They met Daniel in the hall. Yesterday, Janie had had a bit of a crush on him. This morning, she nodded politely and went on her way. What had she seen so appealing about him before? He was a senior, maybe that was it. He seemed almost repugnant today.

She found it hard to concentrate in Professor Wambaugh's class. He had such dreamy blue eyes, and thick blonde hair tied into a ponytail. He was married, but she didn't care. She decided that she was going to have him one way or another. She couldn't understand why he'd married that woman, anyway. She was like Yoko Ono to his John Lennon. Performance art. Huh. She didn't deserve him.

Within a year, her goal had been met. He divorced his wife and married her in the beautiful ceremony she'd always dreamed of. There were parties, interesting people to meet, and her husband adored her. With his income, she was free to pursue her Master's degree. Life was not just good, it was great. She had never been so happy.

It all came to an abrupt end one day with a phone call.

"Mrs. Wambaugh, your husband has been in an accident. You'd better come to Memorial right away."

Joseph was DOA after a drunk driver swerved out of his lane and hit his car head-on. Janie was devastated. She spent the next year grieving; staying at home alone, touching the books and other belongings that he'd left behind, crying. She lost interest in everything.

Finally, after a year had passed, a friend talked her into going to a party. She met Daniel Roberts there, and he began calling. Soon they were dating. At last she decided that she needed to get on with her life. Daniel had been there for her, and they got along pretty well. She didn't really love him, but she didn't expect to ever love another man the way she had Joseph. They were married in a civil service, and went out for beer and pizza afterwards.

They began to bicker almost immediately. Janie's spirit was broken though, and she had no other prospects. Better coming home to argue with Daniel than coming home to an empty house. She dreamed at night of Joseph and the good days. It all seemed like a dream now. Had she ever really been so happy?

They grew old together, she and Daniel, arguing over everything from what movie to rent to which toppings they wanted on their pizza.

Finally one night after thirty years, she had another dream. She immediately recognized the scenario… the crossroads in the moonlight, the dark figure standing before her. She remembered vividly the dream she'd had so long ago, the one she'd managed to forget all these years.

"It's time for you to keep your part of the bargain, Janie."

"What do you mean? You lied to me!"

"I kept my promise. I gave you those things you wanted. I never promised them forever."

"Well, there never was a bargain. I didn't sign any contract."

"Silly woman, your word was your contract. You asked me for help, and I gave it. Now you must come with me."

"But… I never agreed to that!"

"You agreed when you asked for my help. The deal was sealed."

"You lied! You made my life even more miserable by giving me what I wanted and then taking it away!"

She couldn't see him, but she felt a wicked smile in his words.

"I told you that I have many names. One of them is The Father of Lies. Now take my hand, it's time to go."

Unable to resist, she took his hand and followed him into the darkness.

Daniel continued to snore. It would be morning before he found that his wife had died in her sleep.

The Apartment on Church Street

The changes happened so slowly in the beginning that Dylan wasn't even sure they were happening. Maybe that brick building had always been outside his bedroom window. Odd, it looked just like the one from his old apartment; the large and spacious one that he and Cee had shared just a few years ago, before she died.

When he left the bedroom, the bathroom was no longer a short walk across, but down a long hall. Cee's October wreath with its tiny orange lights glowing was at the end of the hall, the bathroom to the left. "I know I'm not dreaming," he thought, "I must be going mad."

Then, the Burger King and the bank building disappeared. He knew that they'd been there, there was no doubt. The view from the living room window was no longer the one he was used to, but Church Street, with its houses lined up across the street below. He was a floor higher than he'd been yesterday.

He didn't mention any of this to his wife, April. She already thought that he was crazy. He raced down the stairs… (Where were the elevators?) and into the street below. He was looking up at his old building, and out at Church Street. When he went back into the building, it had changed. Everything looked older. He raced back up the stairs and into his old apartment. No more blinds covering the windows, there were shades with heavy curtains. The radiators, the Victorian scheme, the French doors which opened into the bedroom… Everything was as it had been. He looked into each room, a wave of nostalgia flowing over him. All he could think of at first was "Damn, it's good to be home."

Then he remembered April. She wasn't anywhere in the house. Neither was Cee. What the hell was going on? He walked over to the computers sitting side by side against the wall. It was the same arrangement as in the new apartment, but the computers themselves were his and Cee's old ones, not the new models he and April had. He'd thrown his old one out recently, and Cee's son had taken hers after her death.

How many times had he wished that he'd kept this old apartment? It was as if the clock had been rewound four years. But he was alone. Slowly it dawned on him that it wasn't the house that he missed so much, but Cee.

He lay down in their old bed and held her pillow close. Without her there, it was only an apartment. One that held many good memories, but still just a place to live now. He thought about April. They had had some good times together too, hadn't they? As he fell asleep, he could hear a voice in his head, saying "You can't live in the past."

He awoke holding April, back in the new apartment.

April was surprised when he kissed her good morning and went into the kitchen to cook their breakfast. He'd been so distant lately that she'd thought about leaving him. Now, for some reason, he was all cheerful and nice.

Dylan found that he could close his eyes and be transported back to his old Church Street apartment anytime he wished, but he was doing it less and less often. Cee wasn't there anymore, but April was here. One day she might not be, and would he be able to forgive himself for being such a lousy husband?

He never told her about his little breakdown, and she never asked what had changed him. They were both just glad that things had changed.

Electric Kool-Aid Kids

Gerald had stopped doing acid after he'd seen Death, but it refused to leave. He was nothing but raw nerve endings now, never sure when death might pop into his mind. A rotting skull in a black robe with maggots writhing in its eye sockets... it wasn't something you wanted to see suddenly appear at random. It never tried to grab him or swipe a scythe at him; it just stood there, grinning. Usually if he looked away for a few seconds, it would be gone. Maybe he was just seeing what others missed; maybe death followed everyone, biding its time, waiting.

He decided that he had to talk to someone about it, but who? The preacher, the school counselor? The doctor? No, he'd have to admit to dropping acid, and they might tell his parents. His buddies wouldn't take him seriously; they'd probably think it was funny. Bunch of morons. They were probably over at Larry's right now, smoking weed and listening to Dark Side Of The Moon cranked up to full volume. "I've always been mad, I've been mad for fucking years." He wondered how it had happened to Syd Barrett. They said the hallucinogens got to him. Maybe they were getting to him, too.

Wendy was the only person he could think of that he could talk about it with. She'd been his girlfriend for a year now, since he was fifteen. She'd been the one he did the acid with, just before a Blue Oyster Cult concert. Maybe she'd understand. He called her and asked her to meet him at Wendy's. It was their favorite burger joint, mainly because of the name, and because it was new. All the kids hung out there now.

They sat down with their fries and cokes. Gerald found it hard to begin. After a long silence, he finally spoke.

"Wendy, remember the acid we did at the BOC concert?

"Of course I do. I've felt closer to you than ever before since then."

"You haven't had any problems with flashbacks, have you?"

She was quiet for a moment.

"You'll think I'm crazy."

"No I won't. Tell me."

"Gerry, I've had the most horrible visions. I never know when I turn a corner if it will be there. It's Death; just like in the horror movies."

Gerald was stunned. She could tell that something was very wrong by the expression on his face.

"Now you'll think I'm crazy, but I've been having that same vision!"

"No, I know you're not crazy. What can we do?"

"I'll be damned if I know. There's no one to go to for help. You have any ideas?"

"No. You're the only person I've told about this."

They both felt a little better just being able to talk about it with each other.

"Maybe it'll just stop sooner or later."

"If it's not sooner, I might lose my mind."

"I know."

Gerald began losing friends. When he stopped doing any drugs, they were suspicious. Some even said he was a narc. He didn't care. He'd lost interest in everything except talking to Wendy. Even then, their main topic of conversation was the times and places they'd seen death.

It was hard to concentrate on schoolwork with the knowledge that Death could appear at any time, grinning that soulless grin. More than once he saw it sitting in the desk next to his. When he looked again, it would be just another kid. It was invading his dreams now as well.

Finally, he broke down and told his mother everything. She'd be more understanding than his father. He didn't have to name names for her to guess that the other person seeing this same thing was Wendy.

"I'm sorry, but this is too important to keep from your father; or from Wendy's parents. I'm going to make you an appointment with a psychiatrist."

She had betrayed him.

Thorazine. Didn't the shrink think it was ironic to treat a drug reaction with drugs? Evidently not. But it seemed to be helping. The flashbacks were coming less often, but Gerald was as nervous as ever. He felt jittery, restless. Wendy's parents had followed suit and taken her to the same psychiatrist. Although he didn't mention it to anyone, Dr. Geoffrey had never seen this before; two people having the exact same psychosis. He asked to see them both on a regular basis.

With the shrink's bag of tricks, Gerald and Wendy made it through the school year of '73-'74 and into summer. The two were as close as only two people who've shared the same life-changing experience can be. Summer dragged. The two had almost no friends. They began haunting an old burger joint that had been popular before Wendy's. It was quieter there, and with less chance of running into former friends. Sometimes Death would join them. He was so familiar now that the fear was almost gone. It was becoming more of a minor annoyance than anything else. Maybe the shrink's drugs were doing it; whatever the case was, they were glad of it.

When school started again, things became even better for them. They were making new friends, and even some of the old ones were back, having decided that they were okay after all. At Halloween, they were invited to a party at one of their new friends' house. Gerald, now sporting a shorter haircut, went as John Kennedy. His father's old suits fit him perfectly. Wendy stuffed her B-cup bra into a D and went as Marilyn Monroe. Her hair was still long, so she stuffed it under a cheap wig. They were the best looking couple at the party. The other kids were costumed from the sublime to the ridiculous. Frankenstein and his bride were dancing beneath a ceiling of orange lights. A witch led her human-sized black cat around on a leash. Dirty Harry was having a heated conversation with Dracula.

Everything started off well, until they noticed one costumed figure who didn't belong. It was their old friend Death. But he wasn't disappearing. He stood alone in a shadowed part of the room, just watching. No one else seemed to notice him. Surely if they had, they'd

have wanted to know who was inside that brilliant costume. Gathering their courage, they decided to go and speak to him. All of this time, and he'd never said a word. If he was going to hang around long enough, they wanted to ask him one question: "Why are you following us?"
Before they could speak, Death did, in a terrible voice that sounded like thousands of voices speaking in unison.

"Don't drink the punch. It's been laced with LSD."

They shivered, but stood their ground.

"Okay, we won't. But why have you been following us?"

"I was told to keep you from harm. You are going to be very important people when you grow up. After tonight, my job is done. I will not visit anymore."

Gerald dreaded hearing that fearful voice again, but he had to ask one more question.

"Why?"

"Had you continued on the path you were on, you would have died tonight. It is not yet your time."

"Good enough for me," he thought.

"Well, what can I say? It's been… horrible."

Death laughed a hollow laugh that somehow reminded them of thousands of bats flying out of a cave.

"Goodbye, Gerald Brown and Wendy Griffin."

Death pulled his disappearing act for the last time. Deciding that they'd had enough Halloween, the two went home. They were in their beds asleep when the fire trucks answered the call to their friend's house. Drinking and drugs, an accidental fire; eight of their classmates were killed that night. The entire town was in shock. Gerald and Wendy were keenly aware of the bullet they'd dodged. They mourned the loss of their friends, but they knew why they had been taken. It was their time. Knowing now that their lives were important, they studied hard and were both given a scholarship to the same excellent school. After college, they were married and went on to do great things, helping many people. I cannot give you more information than this without revealing their true identities. They will tell their story one day on their own, when they are ready. Who am I? The best friend they ever had. We'll meet sooner or later, I promise.

Computer Virus

Artis was doing his usual Saturday night routine, drinking beer and surfing porn. It was getting late, and he was beginning to have to squint to be able to see the naked ladies. He missed the days when you could buy a bottle of ephedrine at any Seven-Eleven. Popping those little white pills he could stay up until he was falling-down drunk. Nowadays, he just started getting sleepy after eight beers or so.

Suddenly a message flashed across his monitor. "You Have a Virus!"

Even half-drunk, he knew that that didn't sound right. Wouldn't his anti-virus program say "Virus Detected?" "Well," he thought, "I've had about enough for tonight anyway. I'll run a virus scan and check it in the morning."

He went to bed unsatisfied, and not drunk enough to fall asleep right away. He prodded his wife Zelda.

"Hey, you awake?"

"No. Leave me alone."

"Your loss, baby."

He felt like talking. Maybe one night he'd try one of those pop-ups that claim to be a woman wishing to talk to you. He knew it was a scam, but he'd never done it. Maybe he would one night just to see what happened.

He awoke slightly groggy the next morning. Once he had a cup of coffee, he sat down at his computer. The scan had completed, and hadn't found any viruses. As he slowly woke up completely, he realized that he felt like crap. "Maybe I do have a virus," he thought. After sitting there for a few minutes doing nothing, he decided to go back to bed.

An hour later, Zelda called out to him.

"Artis, you have to see this!"

The message was flashing on his screen again. This time it said "You Are Very Sick!"

"What have you been looking at, Artis?"

"Nothing unusual, I swear! You know me... I'm not into that kinky stuff."

He told her about the message he'd received the night before.

"Hon, I don't think it's talking about the PC. I think it's talking to me about me. I really do feel sick."

"That's the craziest thing I've ever heard! Are you still drunk?"

"No, I didn't even drink that much last night."

"Go lie back down and I'll get the thermometer."

His fever was at 102 degrees. She put a cold cloth across his forehead and told him that if he wasn't better by morning, he'd have to go to the doctor's office.

Artis was too ill to get out of bed Monday morning. Zelda called his boss and told him that he was sick, then she called the doctor.

"Sounds like a little bug to me. I'll call in some antibiotics for him. You know the rest of the drill; plenty of liquids, rest in bed. If it lasts longer than three days, bring him in."

When she returned from the drugstore, there was another message flashing on his monitor. "You Are Going To Die!"

She ran into the bedroom to check on him. He was wrapped in a blanket, shivering, although his head and face were red with fever. Beads of sweat had formed, but still he shook. She called 911 and waited for the ambulance.

After three days of hell, the fever broke. He was so weak that he needed help walking from his bed to the bathroom. It had been a viral infection, they said. It would take weeks for him to regain his strength.

When he did, the first thing he did was trash the computer.

The Grateful Dead

It was a dark and stormy night. No, really, it was. Thunder rolled, and the sky was lit up intermittently by great flashes of violet. Rain pounded down at a slant from the chill October wind. Miranda walked through the graveyard, holding a black umbrella. It matched her clothing; she looked as though she'd just come from a funeral. There were no recently dead buried here, however. The tombstones were old, lying at crazy angles. The weeds were tall among the high trees. This was her very favorite activity. Late afternoon in autumn was the best, but she'd stayed too long today. She didn't mind the rain or the wind. She felt a sense of peace, of belonging... Far away from the noise and confusion of life, she enjoyed being here, talking to the dead. She knew them all, now. She'd been coming since she was a girl, before she knew that everyone couldn't hear the dead. As she grew older, she learned to keep it to herself. People didn't understand.

Tonight Mr. Witherspoon was complaining that his children never came to see him anymore.

"Mr. Witherspoon, your children are all dead now. They're over at Rolling Hills Cemetery. Next time I'm there, I'll tell them you'd like to hear from them, okay?"

His voice brightened.

"Oh, would you? You're such a sweet girl. It's too bad we can't get up and walk around and visit. But just hearing from them would make me feel so much better. Did they all die of natural causes?"

"All but one. Your youngest son Gary died in an automobile accident."

"Never did trust those newfangled contraptions! If I'd been around, he'd have been riding a horse."

"Things have changed since you left the world. Everyone drives cars now. They're really pretty safe."

"Huh. Not safe enough, I guess."

"I'll have him tell me all about it and give you the message next time I come."

"Okay. I thank you, young lady... where would this bunch here be without you?"

Other voices chimed in, thanking her for her help.

"One day I'm going to figure out how you can get up and walk. I've been studying on it. My great-grandma down in Louisiana was supposed to know how to do it. I'll be leaving soon to visit her old house. Maybe I'll find some answers there."

Miranda said her goodbyes and walked back to her small house in the woods. She knew that in times past she would have been burned as a witch. "Gotta love the New Age," she thought.

A few weeks later, she was in Louisiana. Her great-grandmother's house still stood, isolated from the town. It was unpainted and old, and she knew that she'd better step carefully over the rotting floor boards. There was a book, if she recalled correctly, hidden in the wall somewhere. She'd seen it once when she was very small. It had colorful designs on it that had stayed with her. She knew intuitively that this was the book she needed. Lighting a candle, she began running her fingers over the walls. The house was very dark, and she heard small scurrying's as she stepped lightly and scanned the walls for tell-tale signs.

Finally, behind an old photograph on the wall, she found that a square had been cut out. Reaching inside, she pulled out the dusty old tome. The colors were faded now, but she recognized it. She took it outside into the daylight to get a better look. It was in Latin, with pages of diagrams and strange drawings. She put it carefully away into a leather bag, said goodbye to the house, and began the journey home. "If only I knew where my great-grandma was buried," she thought, "things would be so much easier."

She knew a little Latin, but used the translator on her computer to be sure. The section on raising the dead was not long, but the procedure was complicated. She wondered how much of it was really necessary and how much was just for show. The Old Ones had always been big on showiness. She studied for hours, her black cat with its black eyes studying her. There were warnings about doing it, that sometimes what came out of the ground was not quite what had gone in. She smiled thinking of all the horror stories that she'd read on the subject. "The dead deserve freedom as much as anyone," she thought. "They want the same things the living do; love, companionship, something to keep them busy." How tedious it must be to lie stuck in the ground day in and day out.

"...beneath a full moon, draw a pentagram in the dirt with a sharp stick. Place a black male cat in the center. Do the incantation to make him human for twenty-four hours. He must be the one to read the incantation for the raising of the dead…"

"How's your Latin, Mr. Pibb?" she asked, stroking her cat.

By the next full moon she was ready. Mr. Pibb made a striking young Black man. Miranda was sorry the spell would only last a day. He read from the book with no trouble, after telling her he preferred the Friskies to that damned generic brand of cat food she bought sometimes.

After the brief ceremony, they heard a rumbling in the ground. It was a sound unlike any other they'd ever heard. Mr. Pibb loped off back home to hide under the bed. Suddenly, the thirty or so graves opened up, and there they stood. All of her dead friends, dressed in their Sunday best. They weren't decayed in moldy rags, but looked to be in their prime. You'd never know that they were dead to look at them. "That's some powerful magic!" she thought.

They were grateful to her for releasing them, but soon began asking where they could go for a little drinking and dancing. Their arms and legs were stiff, and they all walked around trying to get loosened up.

"Party at your place?"

"Oh, no, my house is much too small. I don't keep any alcohol anyway."

"Which way to town? Oh, wait, I remember now. Come on, everyone, let's go party!"

"Mr. Witherspoon! I'm surprised at you! I thought that you'd want to go see your family."

"They'll be there tomorrow. Sure ain't going anywhere!"

The sight of all these people in their old-fashioned suits and dresses heading for town made her wonder if she'd done the right thing. It wasn't what she'd expected. Still, she had the rest of the night before Mr. Pibb changed back into a cat. She went home with the intention of coaxing him out from under the bed and into it.

They were all back the next day, knocking on her door.

"We're ready to go back to the cemetery."

"But why? All you ever talked about was getting out."

"This is not our world anymore. The things we saw last night! Indecent gyrations under colored lights, some kind of noise that passes for music now… weak beer or fancy sweet drinks… everyone thought we were some kind of foreigners. The cars, the crowds, the whole city has changed. We've had enough."

"I don't know how to reverse the spell, but I have an idea."

She led them all back to the graveyard, holding a shotgun. With each dead person standing beside their own grave, she shot them one by one. As each dropped back in, they said "Thank you."

Back home, she began searching through her great-grandmother's book for a spell to make a cat human permanently. It was odd to see a grown man eating from a bowl on the floor, but she was sure he'd adapt in time. Besides, he had the most beautiful black eyes…

The Dream Police

The world was spinning too fast, and Jim knew that he was going to be thrown off. A flock of porcupines flew by like the winged monkeys of Oz. Colors swirled until they mixed together and everything turned the color of mud. Trees laughed as they were uprooted, freed from their monotonous standing. Someone whispered in his ear… "You're in the wild, wild, west now, baby." He awoke, breathing hard, behind the wheel of his ancient Pinto. Horns were honking at him as he pulled back into the proper lane. The narcoleptic episodes were becoming more frequent, and he was worried.

Janice popped a couple of painkillers without water. She was used to it, now, but she couldn't get used to the pain in her back. It felt like knives twisting into her. The pills always made her sleepy, but there was nothing else she could do to ease the pain. She lay down on the bed and waited for them to kick in. A 'Scrubs' re-run was on TV. "Who put the silverware in the pancakes drawer?" It was still funny every time. She wondered if she would go back inside that guy's head when she slept. She didn't want to, it must be terribly inconvenient for him. Still, it was fun to whisper crazy things in his ear. Did he remember them when he woke up? "You're not in Kansas anymore, baby. Welcome to the big time." Janice watched a lot of TV.

Jim sat at his desk, attempting to write poetry. Why did he keep thinking about 'Scrubs'?

A long line of black limos, white orchids, organ music. Cartoon skeletons appeared and began dancing in a chorus line. Someone tapped him on the shoulder, and he woke up. His wife Selena, with a worried look on her face.

"You fell asleep at your desk again."

"Goddamnit."

"When are the results from the CT scan supposed to be back?"

"Dr. NaJeeb is supposed to call, probably today or tomorrow."

She ran her fingers through his hair and kissed him on the back of his head.

"It'll be all right, I'm sure of it."

Dr. NaJeeb looked worried. Sitting across his desk from them, he opened his mouth to speak twice before any words came out.

"Jim, I'm going to put this as well as I'm able. You have a woman in your head."

Now it was Jim's turn to be speechless.

"A… what? A woman? What do you mean, Doctor?"

"Basically, she visits you when she sleeps. This causes you to fall asleep. I've only heard of one case of this before, I wasn't sure it was even real until I looked it up."

"I have several colleagues at work on this already. Would you consider going into the Dream Unit in Mayfield for a week or so?"

"Jesus H Christ! Selena?"

"I think you have to, Jim. What other options are there?"

The doctor answered.

"There are no other options. I cannot treat this either at home or in a regular hospital. I can't even assure you that this will work. Think it over and call me when you decide. But I have to warn you, if left untreated your situation is only going to become worse."

"Have you any idea who this woman is?"

"That's the first thing we're going to try and find out."

Jim didn't hesitate.

"We're in. No need to think about it. Give us a day to put everything on hold for a week."

Dr. NaJeeb nodded.

"Maybe you should make it two."

Janice was feeling more at home each time she visited the man. She wondered what it would be like to be him, to live his life, think his thoughts. She could tell that he was young and fit, and didn't have all the pain that she was burdened with. She wondered… "What if I didn't wake up? Could I live inside him always? What odd thoughts I'm having. Maybe it's the new medicine."

She fed the cat, ate a frozen dinner, and lay down to watch TV. Lucy and Ethel were in trouble again. She drifted away into sleep. She knocked on her friend's door, but was denied entry. He was probably in deep REM sleep. She wouldn't have any fun tonight. She woke up long enough to turn the channel to 'Seinfeld' and went straight back to sleep.

The Dream Unit was much smaller than Jim and Selena had expected. It was an attachment to Mayfield General, unmarked. It was almost as though the hospital was ashamed of having it on the property. The inside was dimly lit compared to the usual bright hospital lights. Only a few staff members manned the place. It seemed to be very conducive to sleep. Inside Jim's room, electrodes were attached to his head, chest and fingers. They were going to take some getting used to. Various monitors lined one side of the wall.

Dr. Pomalbaum entered the room when all was ready. He explained that everything would be recorded twenty-four hours per day. They would first try to establish his normal sleep patterns, and then see if there was a pattern to the disturbances. Jim felt as though he were already in a dream. All he could do now was to wait until he fell asleep, whether normally or by a narcoleptic episode.

There were beasts howling in the darkness, their red eyes glowing. An old lady on a broom rode the sky, writing out the words "Surrender, Jim" with smoke from the broom. Then he was walking through a field of poppies, getting very tired and sleepy… He heard his own voice, reciting a poem.

"These are the days of the colorless sky, of pale nights and undreamt dreams…"

"If only," he thought.

Janice jiggled the knob to Jim's mind and found it open. When she entered, red light was flashing over a serene landscape. She could hear the opening music to 'Sanford and Son' in the distance. Her TV. Louder were the bleeps and blips coming from inside. She twirled and danced happily, no pain here to keep her from it. Maybe she'd go rock climbing. "Look!" she thought, "a playground with swings! It's so nice here. All I have at home is Cat Fred and the TV. Maybe I will just stay. I wonder what will happen if I do?"

Jim wasn't waking up. The monitors were going wild, but he remained in deep sleep. He heard someone say "He's dreaming." But he wasn't… was he? He could see the room, the monitors, Selena… he could see himself lying on the bed, all wired up. A familiar voice whispered in his ear. "Everything old is new again, baby." He began to panic. He was outside of himself and didn't know how to get back in. What was that? "…variation of established pattern…" "…slipped into a coma…" "We have to get her out of there…" "Jim! Jim! Wake up!" He watched as a doctor gave him a shot in the neck.

Floating down from the ceiling, he crawled into his own ear canal. He was back in. An old woman was swinging on a swing set, with red light flashing all around.

"Welcome to surreal city, baby."

"You can't be here. Go home."

"La-dee-da-dee-dah, I can't hear you."

As he began walking in her direction, he found himself travelling through a maze of buildings. He walked through a Chinese family's house to reach the other side. They sat eating dinner, ignoring him. He walked through an old deserted factory, hearing a sound like water dripping in a cave. He walked up and down stairs and fire escapes, trying to reach the place he'd come in. Finally, there was an open field, as large as several football fields; far away he could see the flashing red lights. He began running, a hot wind blowing against his back. He heard a sound like a laugh track on an old television sitcom. It receded as he gained ground. Then it actually was a football field, with dead football players dancing to Harry Belafonte's 'Jump in the Line.' No matter how fast he ran, he didn't seem to be getting any closer. He could see her there, swinging and smiling sweetly at him, but now he was running in mud. "The placebo is having no effect," he thought, and couldn't help but laugh. Selena and Dr. Pomalbaum were looking down from the sky, singing 'White Rabbit.'

Suddenly, there was a sound like a loud rapping on a door. Looking around, he saw that there *was* a door.

"Open up! Dream Police!"

The door was kicked in, and two large white-helmeted men in black uniforms appeared. They went over to the old lady and grasped her under each arm.

"C'mon, lady, let's go. You can't be in here."

She begged and wheedled, then cursed loudly as they began carrying her out.

Once she was gone, the red lights stopped flashing, and the dream world became beautiful and peaceful. A couple of maintenance men were installing a new steel door in place of the one that had been kicked down. Jim awoke. A doctor was removing the wires.

"Is it over? Am I cured?"

"Yes, we found the problem. You shouldn't have any more narcoleptic episodes. I've given your wife my card, just in case."

Selena hugged him tightly. He'd been asleep for eight days.

Janice was found dead in her bed by the landlord. It was determined that she'd taken an accidental overdose of her pain medication. The TV was on, a sad episode of MASH with no laugh track.

Andy and the Grits

In northwestern Washington State stands a small casino/resort called Little Creek. It became famous for hosting Baby boomer bands, attracting not just the Boomers but people of all ages. When Gary Puckett and the Union Gap cancelled their show for the night, the crowd showed their disappointment by stomping their feet, shouting obscenities and throwing beer bottles from all directions. They only got louder when it was announced over the speaker that Andy and the Grits would be the replacement band. It was not what they'd come to hear. They did quiet down to some extent when the lights went out and a thick fog rose from the stage, like the fog in dark cemeteries at midnight

A booming voice from above announced to the crowd "Everyone please welcome Andy and The Grits."

"Boo.....boo!" was heard everywhere, but the young singer was not rattled.

"Thank you," yelled Andy, "We'd like to start off the evening with an original tune."

"Play Wipeout," screamed a high-pitched woman in her late thirties.

"Get off the stage," slurred a man who unfortunately had front-row seats.

A half-empty beer bottle whizzed past Andy's' ear. Ignoring it, he blasted out the first chords of the new song. The crowd began to quiet down as the other instruments joined in, a solid rock beat in minor chords. Even the cocktail waitresses stopped to stare for a moment. None of them had heard music like this before. It soared and wailed; the chant-like chorus soon had then all singing and clapping along.

"I dreamed I was in the deep dark sea/ drowning, drowning, drowning"

Andy; a common name, given to a blonde baby boy who never cried. He never made a sound until at the age of two when he shocked his parents by quietly and in perfect pitch began to sing his favorite lullaby. From then on Andy sang more than he talked. He seemed to seek refuge in a secret world all his own. Andy's blonde hair never changed; he grew into a charismatic youth who never seemed to notice the girls who adored him from afar and became his fans when he started his own band in the garage of his parents' home.

Tonight Andy was dressed in red pin-striped pants and a black turtleneck sweater that made the peace sign necklace that hung around his neck shine in the spotlight. Andy's' band members were also dressed in what resembled the 60's, so the Baby Boomers loved it. Andy sensed that he had by then captivated the crowd. His lyrics mesmerized them as he sang the refrain, "I dreamed I was in the deep dark sea, drowning, drowning, drowning." After half a dozen repeats with his new fans singing along, he dropped his guitar and picked up a violin. After what seemed like an eternity he sang to a by then impatient crowd, "I dreamed, yes I dreamed, I dreamed, yes I dreamed." The reaction of the crowd was a first in this tiny casino out of nowhere; they could be heard by all of the distant farmhouses and even at the town's one gas station.

Not knowing what to expect next from Andy kept the crowd standing, as if they didn't dare sit and miss one beat. In the middle of the singing and clapping the stage suddenly went black, the fog rose and Andy appeared through the fog shirtless, his peace sign radiant around his neck. His slow, captivating song, "The deep dark sea, deep dark sea," lyrics that only repeated themselves began to puzzle his audience, but they soon joined in, as if in a trance.

Just as the crowd was beginning to clap along with the lyrics one more, the music stopped. The silence crawled under everyone's skin for what seemed an eternity. Finally, Andy grabbed the microphone, closed his eyes and made strange sounds, ocean sounds. The crowd went into a frenzy, unable to duplicate the strange and haunting sounds he was making. They were only able to repeat as loud as they could, "Drowning, drowning, drowning." Andy had managed to take the crowd into the ocean with him; soon they were unable to take their eyes off of him as they fought for air. Most of them were feeling like they were going under, where they did not know; somewhere with Andy, though, and so it did not matter to them. Andy started to close and yet they yelled for more. He had taken them to somewhere strange, cold and frightening, yet they continued to beg him not to stop. When Andy's sounds changed to a moaning low groan, to everyone's dismay the lights came back on. Andy was wearing his sweater once more and he and his band broke into a more upbeat song, "Who Do

You Love." Andy realized what an effect he had on his audience and knew he had to stop. It was almost a relief, but not quite.

In spite of changing the atmosphere, the percussion was driving into the brains of the crowd. It was too late; a strange mood had overcome the room, the people on the farms and the gas attendant. Something was in their brains, feeding off of their energy. After thirty minutes of more light-hearted music, Andy and the Grits left the stage for the headliners to set up. Andy's last song was another original, "Wormwood Star." The audience loved the song so much they wouldn't stop screaming until Andy came out for an encore. Finally the fog rose from the stage as the band disappeared. What was left after the fog rose were row after row of cemetery headstones. No one realized, but the name of each of the band members was carved into the headstones.

Fatal Karma played a good long set, but the crowd did not really hear them; their minds were somewhere else. Andy's' strange music had crawled into their heads and wouldn't leave.

Walking home from the concert, Karen and Peter from the front row felt for the first time an uneasy feeling coming from somewhere in the darkness. They walked faster than usual. Karen screamed as she thought she was looking in the gutter at a dog being eaten by a million maggots. Peter forced Karen's' hands from her eyes to show her that there was nothing in the gutter. She was finally able to convince herself that she was only reacting to Andy's song, yet still hastened her walk home. Peter was always telling her she had an overactive imagination, so once more he'd proved himself right. Or so they thought. Peter acted brave but did not feel it. He felt a cold breeze through his thick coat in spite of the fairly warm night. Their friends, Alexia and Patrick, tried to catch up to them, but they had already disappeared in their hurry to get home.

Peter, Karen, Alexia and Patrick weren't the only ones spooked by images or thoughts of maggots, nor could they ignore smelling what seemed to be ocean smells, although they were too far away to smell water of any kind. Everyone who had been to hear Andy dreamed of worms that night. Most of them were friends, so it didn't take long to compare notes the following day. They definitely had people talking now. By the next Friday night, there was a huge crowd in the small casino concert hall waiting to hear them sing once more. The local DJ, DJ Dick, had caught the buzz and was there as well. There was no booing this time, only a hushed, almost fearful silence as Andy and his band took the stage.

44

Andy once more introduced himself and The Grits for a second week in a row. This time the crowd's clapping seemed nervous and somewhat stifled in anticipation of what lay ahead. Soon though, they were launching into a thirty minute jam of "Wormwood Star," closing with an extra fifteen minutes of "Drowning." The crowd came to hear them and only them, so half the people left after the first set, not waiting to hear the Muscletones, another Baby Boomer band.

DJ Dick caught them backstage and invited them to be interviewed on his show. They politely declined. Dick had never heard of any band passing on the chance for self-promotion, especially some little-known band. Who were these guys? After hearing Andy, Dick dreamed of interviewing worms on his radio show, worms with faces like the bands'. All through the night Dick woke up drenched in sweat, his heart pounding. He ordinarily loved his job, loved relating to people. He'd been a wall-flower all through school, his face laden with untreated acne, along with being slightly obese. He had been a loner struggling after bouts of depression. As a DJ he had hoped that being around people he would climb out of his self-made abyss. With the arrival of Andy and the Grits, Dick suddenly had an interest completely revolving around everything concerning Andy, the band, and what made them tick. Instead of his usual dreams of hooking worms on the end of his fishing pole, he woke up with a chill after dreaming of the worms in his fishing can multiplying and spilling over onto the ground. These worms, like the others, seemed to be in a feeding frenzy. They sent chills down his spine as they would occasionally stop and stare at him, looking straight through his eyes.

Two hours later he finally jumped out of bed, turned on every light in his home, loaded up his small revolver and sat up in his chair until fat last the morning light flooded his kitchen. It all seemed so surreal now.

That night everyone who had heard Andy and The Grits dreamed of worms again. By the next weekend they were headlining at a bigger nightspot. People were trying to figure out who they were, where they were from. Definitely not local, they knew. In an age of information, no one could seem to find out anything at all about them. It was a well-known fact by now that their music would give you strange dreams. There was a big buzz about this little band, but no one even knew where they were living.

No good photographs of them even existed, just the cell phone shots from a dark hall. The phone number the club managers had for them were disposable cell phones. They had no manager; Andy handled all of the bookings himself.

With the help of a friend at the police department, Dick managed to finally find out some information. These guys were obviously pulling off some huge publicity stunt. Andy Wainright had been the leader of an up-and-coming band called The Gift. Their plane crashed in 1969, and all six members were killed. When the plane crashed into the Pacific, the ocean claimed three. The other three bodies floated to a nearby deserted island. Devoured by maggots, they were never found.

Dick thought to himself, "These guys are smart, but what about the drowning throat sounds that came from Andy on stage, and what about the worms? How are they pulling this off?" It would haunt him the rest of his life. Andy and The Grits disappeared as quickly as they had come. The dreams subsided, and Little Creek returned to normalcy. He didn't know that in another dark concert hall somewhere they were taking the stage and the audience once more.

The next time you find yourself in a small dark casino bar, don't be surprised if you find yourself clapping along with the beat from a young, charismatic singer wearing a gold peace sign around his neck. Lights dim as Andy sings in his softest voice, as if to you alone.

"I sang you a song my friends

I sang it soft and low

I sang it for you my friends

And now I have to go."

House of Dreams

1

Out through the fields of tall weeds and wild grasses, past a decayed oak and a rusted-out pick-up truck; into the dense woods on the other side, where the ground is carpeted by multiple layers of dead leaves built up over a century; there stands an old house, its boards grey and weather-beaten. At night, flickering blue lights dance through the darkness, but there is no one there to see…

On a steaming day in July, the air heavy and hard to breathe, insects of two dozen varieties filled the thick air, thrown into a frenzy from the heat. The drone of their buzzing had become background noise. I was totally focused on the warped, weathered boards of the old house. Specks of white paint still clung stubbornly in places. A two-story Southern Gothic masterpiece, it had been abandoned now for many years. Overgrown with weeds and briars, it fairly vibrated with memories of long-ago days… Lives lived and lost, children's laughter, the sounds of cooking, whispered secrets; all the mundane moments that fill our lives between the great joys and tragedies. Memories hung in and around the house like spirits, not yet ready to leave this world, wanting to mean more than they had in their short lives. I felt a deep and mournful sense of loss, for what I wasn't sure.

A sudden wind arose, roaring through the leaves of the trees overhead. Disturbed birds flapped madly as huge raindrops began to fall. Quickly, I sought shelter in the house. I cannot say that I thought quickly; I did not think. I just did it. The door was ajar, and before I knew it I was inside. It was dark and damp, but not as hot as I'd expected. The wind blew through the windows, tattered curtains flying. I was surprised to see that it was still furnished with ancient furniture; bookshelves with half-crumbled books, ornate tables with dusty vases that once held flowers. It was full of dust and debris, dead leaves scattered everywhere. There was a huge fireplace near the center of the far wall, and a door beside it that led down a hallway. Something gleamed in the fireplace. Something white. A bone? No, many tiny bones. As I watched, they assembled themselves into the form of something like a possum and scurried down the hallway. Suddenly I felt very sleepy, and had to lie on the dusty old sofa to keep from falling to the floor. I dreamed of tiny blue lights hovering around my head, talking to me. I dreamed of plague doctors crawling the walls like spiders. I dreamed of a foreign land with strange beings walking strange streets, all in the most vivid colors. The blue lights were soothing, comforting; I didn't feel in danger. In fact, I felt exhilarated. I belonged here. I didn't want to leave the house, these dreams. I wanted to stay forever.

I was late for dinner, but my wife was used to that. My mood surprised her; I'm not usually the most demonstrative of men, but I took her in my arms and gave her a soulful kiss. She didn't even mention my tardiness. Later that night we made passionate love for the first time in weeks. I knew that she wondered what had come over me, but would never ask. She knew that she'd married a strange man, and was just happy that I was happy for a change.

By the next day my mood had changed again. I felt anxious, unfulfilled. My mind kept wandering back to the house. By early afternoon, I found myself walking trance-like back in its direction. It was there waiting, like an old friend. I wanted to explore more of it, but the drowsiness came over me almost as soon as I entered. The strange little creature from yesterday gave a repeat performance. I felt that it wanted me to follow, but I was so sleepy… Soon I was back on the sofa in body and in the strange land in spirit. There was something very familiar about those twisted streets. I seemed to know my way around as I walked. Odd-looking people greeted me as we passed as though they knew me. I returned their greetings without hesitation. This land of green skies seemed somehow to be home, more than my own world had ever been.

I walked into a curio shop and bought a wolf's head walking cane. I didn't need money; my pockets were full of gold dust. The blue lights kept me company, always hovering about my head. I was headed for a little pub called The Dreamhouse, sandwiched in between a library and a café. Just before I reached the door, I felt a little tug. Suddenly I was awake on the old sofa, holding my new walking cane. I'd brought it out of my dream! Even though I hadn't stayed as long as I'd have liked, I was filled once again with that feeling of happiness and well-being. I walked home in the darkness, whistling a tune that I'd never heard before. At least not in this world.

2

My sixty-fifth summer passed quickly. I began visiting the house earlier each day so that I could spend more time there. I always seemed to wake soon after dark. I wasn't getting any writing done, and my wife's happiness had turned to worry. I'd lost some weight, despite eating the oddly comforting food in Dreamland. I knew that if I wasn't being pushed out somehow, I'd never leave. But every night I'd awake, feeling refreshed, and walk back to what I wasn't really sure *was* my home anymore. I loved my wife dearly, but things were changing. I was changing. The pull of the house began to wake me during the night. I wanted to tell her about it all, but was sure that she'd start a campaign to make me see a psychiatrist. I wished that I could take her with me, just once. Then she'd see.

Slowly I began to realize why the Dreamland peoples' faces were all so familiar. They were people I'd known who had died. This shook me a bit, and I decided not to go back. At least not for a while. But the air was so mysteriously sweet there, the green skies always clear... One night I awoke with an overwhelming urge to visit the house. It was October, the night air chilly. I slipped quietly out of bed, dressed and put on my jacket. Nothing had ever happened at night there before, but the urge to go was so strong that I had no choice. Leaving my sleeping wife, I left, closing the door gently behind me. The woods were strange in the moonlight; nocturnal creatures scurried in the bush and shadows danced. I had no trouble finding my way. The path I'd made was well-worn now.

I didn't become overwhelmed with sleepiness this time as I entered. I was at last able to follow the small creature down the hall and open the door. It opened to the street scenes of Dreamland, stars twinkling in the green sky. I was entering fully conscious this time. It was thrilling and intimidating at once. Everything appeared much clearer, the colors more vivid. The faces of the people were all clearer now; I recognized them all. I was home. They all knew me, and came out to hug me and pat my back.

"We thought you'd never make it!" someone said. It was my father.

"But what about Samantha? I can't leave her behind."

"She'll be along soon enough, I promise. Welcome home!"

I was pulled away into the merriment of The Dreamhouse, feeling better than I had in many years.

After three days had passed, the circling buzzards overhead led them to my body. The room at the end of the hallway was an old green kitchen. I sat at the table, face down on my arm, resting. I was sorry to see my wife's tears, but I knew Father was right. She'll be here soon. She'll love it here, like we all do.

The Violet World

1

"Our lives are but stories, told to entertain the gods" - unknown

Celeste was happy with her new "studio." It was actually the second-largest bedroom in the new house, but it was large enough for everything she needed. Her computer desk, an easel, a table for paints, brushes and other supplies. Bookshelves against the wall full of art books. A stuffed owl and an artist's mannequin topped the bookshelf, along with various shells she'd collected. She wondered what she'd do if she had to choose between art and James. As much as she loved him, it would be a tough call.

James was her husband, a writer. The smallest bedroom suited his needs. He wrote magazine articles while working on his short stories and The Novel. They had both been doing well lately, and finally were able to afford the new house in Scotland County. They worked all day in their own little worlds, but at night there was a large living room and master bedroom. Both of them being workaholics, they regretted not spending more time there, but it was hard for either of them to stop once they got on a roll. Sometimes they'd work late into the night, and end up too tired to do anything but flop down and sleep.

They were basically happy. They had their morning coffee time together. Sometimes she'd cook breakfast; sometimes he'd make (according to him) his world-famous omelets. Other than that, they ate a lot of pizza and Chinese delivery. Maybe one day, they thought, they'd be able to afford a cook/housekeeper. But for now, they were essentially happy. This was so much better than the cramped apartment they'd shared in Illinois. "Ill-a-noise," James called it. It was quiet here in the country. Sometimes it seemed too quiet. It had actually been scary-quiet those first couple of weeks, but they were becoming used to it now.

Celeste stared intently at the painting she was working on. It was a surreal piece; she was attempting to depict the passing of time. She'd painted a door in the center, closed. Now it was cracked open. She couldn't comprehend it. She *knew* that she'd painted it closed. "It's late," she thought. She cleaned her brushes and went to bed. She could hear James' keyboard tapping as she passed his office, so she didn't disturb him.

She told him about it the next morning. They both laughed, and he told her she should take a break. "Go ride your bicycle, get some air." She did just that. It was a beautiful day, although a little hot and muggy.

She picked up a few things from the grocery store, deciding to cook dinner. A real meal, with pork chops, collard greens and sweet potatoes. Maybe she'd even make some cornbread. But first, she wanted to look at the painting.

Celeste froze in front of the easel, her eyes growing wide. The door was a bit more open now. And… she could swear she saw things moving inside. She stood there transfixed, unable to speak or even move. She couldn't be dreaming, she *knew* she was awake. She wanted to call out for James, but couldn't. A finger inside the door had just given the signal for her to come in.

Finally she managed to avert her eyes. Closing the studio door behind her, she went into the kitchen and began making dinner. Her mind wasn't on the food, though; what she'd saw…or at least what she *thought* she saw… kept roiling over in her mind.

She didn't tell James. She was wondering if she was on the verge of some sort of breakdown. She picked at her meal while James happily downed his and went back for more.

"Leave the dishes, baby, I'll get them in the morning. I'm too full to do anything now but go to bed."

"Thanks, James. I'm right behind you."

He was snoring in less than five minutes. Sleep didn't come so easily for her. When she did finally drift off, she had the strangest dream. She was inside the painting. She knew that somehow. There was an entire world in there, a different world. The skies were violet and sparkled with yellow stars. Things moved in the darkness, shadows that she couldn't quite see. There was dark vegetation of some sort everywhere, and the shadows seemed to be moving behind it. She noticed ferns taller and wider than herself. And music... there was an alien music playing, like she'd never heard before. She couldn't discern the instruments used. Something flute-ish, maybe. An odd rhythm of some type of percussion instrument, but nothing she'd ever heard.

She awoke at five AM, unrested. She did her morning routine like a zombie. The dream didn't want to shake out of her head. The sound of her doing the dishes awoke James. He walked in, sleepy-eyed.

"I told you that I'd get them."

"That's okay, baby, I needed something to do. The coffee's ready."

"Are you okay? You don't look so great."

"Maybe I'm coming down with something. I didn't sleep well last night."

As they sat in their breakfast nook drinking coffee, she couldn't hold back any longer. She told him about the painting, the dream, everything.

He frowned. "I believe that dreams are sometimes your subconscious trying to tell you something. Are you worried about something? Maybe it's just that you're still trying to adjust to a new place."

"No, if that were the case it would be *you* having the dreams. I grew up here."

"You've been away a long time though. Everything old is new again."

"James, I swear I'm afraid to go look at that painting. I know that I painted a closed door. What if it's open?"

"Come on, I'll go with you. Maybe you're just nervous about the show in Chicago."

They walked like children approaching a haunted house. When they stood in front of the easel, the door was half-open.

"You *sure* you didn't paint it like this?"

She shook her head.

"Well, paint over it and make sure it's closed. Do it right now, so I can see it."

She did.

They both worked the rest of the day. The painting with the door was finished, with the door definitely closed.

Celeste didn't work late that night; she was overcome with the need to sleep. She stopped by James' office on her way to bed.

"I'm going to bed, baby. Can you get your own dinner?"

"Don't worry, I'm not hungry. I have to get this piece out for The New Yorker before the deadline. Sweet dreams... I'll even let you dream about Jeff Bridges."

She laughed, hugged him from the back and went to bed.

Within minutes, she was back in the Violet World. This time, she noticed that there were stairs... 112 of them, she somehow knew. There was an object at the top that she couldn't quite make out. She began climbing the stairs. When she finally reached the top, she could see that the object was a battered old suitcase. It was locked, and she didn't see a key. "What am I supposed to do now?"

"Wake up! You're having a bad dream!"

"Huh? Oh, James! I was there again!"

She jumped out of bed naked and ran down to her studio. The painting

was still on the easel. The door was half-way open. James was right behind her. He looked with disbelief.

"You didn't re-paint that door?"

"No, I swear I didn't!"

"Damn. Just... damn. Maybe you're getting up and painting in your sleep."

"No way. I spent most of my night climbing stairs."

"I think we should take it out to the backyard and burn it!"

"No!" she didn't even know why she said it, but she was adamant about keeping it.

An eerie violet glow shone through the half-open door.

She remembered her grandmother from South Carolina, who was rumored to be a witch. "Explain this to me, Granny" she whispered softly.

2

Neither of them tried to work that day. They had a good meal, showered together, and made love for what seemed like the first time in weeks. As she lay nestled in his arms staring at the ceiling, she actually *wanted* to go to sleep. There was something there that she needed to know.

When she entered the Violet World this time, there were a series of doors, one beside each three steps. "The key to that suitcase is in one of these doors", she thought. "I have to *know*."

She approached the first door and opened it. Suddenly she was outside on a bright hot summer day. There was a little blonde girl holding her hand, pulling on her.

"C'mon, Mommy! Ice cream! Ice cream!" She looked down at her own arm. Her ebony arm had turned white. She heard the jingle of an ice cream truck, and let herself be led to it by her eager (daughter?) She pulled out a change purse and paid the man, an elderly gentleman. They walked up the drive to a small house. Celeste heard herself say "Sit out here on the porch and eat your ice cream, you'll make a mess inside." Inside the house was a shock. It looked like something out of the 1930s or '40s. No TV or computer, a large radio was the centerpiece of the living room. She turned it on, and heard them announce that the president was about to speak. President Franklin Delano Roosevelt. Suddenly air raid sirens went off, screaming at the world.

The little girl came in and said "Mommy, we have to go in the basement."

"You go ahead, dear, I'll be right there."

Once the girl was gone, she sped for the door as fast as she could in the heels that she was wearing in here. She closed the door on the summer and the sirens, and was herself again. Tee-shirt, jeans, running shoes, and most definitely Black. "I've had enough of this for now" she thought, and woke up. It was seven AM, and she could smell the coffee.

"It was the most incredible thing I've ever experienced! I was someone else, but I was still *me*! I knew where everything was in that house, it was all familiar! I knew that little girl was my daughter!"

"What house? What little girl? What are you trying to tell me?"

She told him everything that she'd seen and done. "I was me, but another me. A me that belonged to another time. I had this powerful sense of déjà vu the entire time I was in there."

"We'll have to worry about this when you get back from Chicago. You have a show to hang. Maybe it'll all go away after that. Maybe it's just anxiety." He didn't even believe it himself as he spoke the words.
"I have one more night here before I have to leave. I want to see this thing through."

"Damn a bunch of crazy-ass women."

The terrain was beginning to seem familiar. Celeste decided to take a quick peek into the first door she'd entered yesterday. There was a cold rain falling from gray skies. There seemed to be a graveside funeral going on just up ahead. She quickly closed the door. She'd seen the little girl dressed in black among the mourners.

She tried to open the next door just a crack, but it swung open and she was in before she knew what was happening. She was on her stomach behind a rock, holding a rifle with a bayonet attached. Her hands, she saw, were a dark ebony. She was wearing a blue uniform. It was night, but there were blasts that lit up the sky with red. She looked at her hands again and realized that these were the hands of a man. Suddenly a shout sounded out. "Go, go, go, we got these damn rebels on the run!" She jumped up and ran with the other soldiers, chasing a rag-tag army of what must have been Confederate soldiers. She didn't have to think what to do, she just did. The soldier ahead of her got close enough to an enemy to run him through with his bayonet. "No prisoners!" he shouted. "The only good rebel is a dead one. Kill 'em all!" She felt a rage that she'd never felt before through this man that she was now. She was running, killing anything that wasn't wearing blue. Suddenly she was running through a door, and was back in the Violet World. She was shaking, still feeling the rage. It took her several minutes to calm down and feel like herself again.

While Celeste was busy preparing for her next show, James began reading up on the space time continuum theories, trying to explain to himself what had happened. Evidently, she'd literally opened a door, somehow. But through a painting? He couldn't make sense of it. Never a left-brain thinker, all of this sounded like crunching metal to him. He had a friend in Florida who might be able to explain it to him, but how would he even go about asking? And what of the supernatural? James had never believed in anything he couldn't see, but what if there was something there after all? Maybe the supernatural was just a matter of physics that hadn't been explained yet. Something had happened, whatever it was. These were no ordinary dreams.

After Celeste had supervised the hanging of her show and done the obligatory social events, she was itching to go back to her easel. All of these people in there were her, in other forms, in other lives. She had the rarest of opportunities, and she didn't want to waste it. She'd never thought much about reincarnation, but that seemed to be what she was dealing with here. Plus, behind one of those doors was a key...

Back at home with James, she waited anxiously for sleep to come. She no longer feared the watching shadows. The Violet World with its strange music had become familiar, even friendly, to her. Tonight there were pennies on the ground at the bottom of the stairs. She knew it was a sign, but what?

Several doors down, she noticed one with smoke curling out from around its edges. Standing in front of it, she could hear sounds. Sounds like helicopters, like babies crying, like the moans of the dying. She dreaded opening this door, but she felt that this was the one that held the key.

In her dream, she sat down on the bottom step to think, and had a vision; a dream within a dream. She saw a stack of envelopes tied together with red ribbon. The key, she knew, was beneath them. She also heard the name Malcolm clearly spoken. She became angry, and woke herself up muttering "Nothing makes sense here". It was time to get up anyway. She let James sleep while she made the coffee.

Later, she began a new painting, depicting the Violet World. The door on the old one was wide open.

She went to bed late that night; James was already asleep. When she "awoke" inside the dream, she was still sitting on the step contemplating everything that had happened. She knew that she must open the door with the smoke seeping out around its edges. She steeled herself for whatever might happen and opened it.

There was no sense of déjà vu this time; she was completely in the moment. She was a Red Cross nurse, in a chopper with her partner Malcolm. They were landing in an African village where the soldiers had just been through with their guns and machetes. Smoke was everywhere. The destruction of property seemed like nothing compared to the destruction of people. There has never been a war movie or even a horror movie to depict the suffering and bloodshed in that small village. More choppers landed, and they all worked feverishly to try to save the wounded.

Some of the soldiers returned and began attacking the medical workers. She was forced by her own people into a chopper, still unwilling to abandon the wounded. She screamed for Malcolm, but she couldn't see him. Then they were rising into the air, and she fell out of the door.

Celeste gasped for breath from the smoke, sitting with her back to the door. She wanted to rush back in and find Malcolm. It took her a long time to recover her senses, and when she did she couldn't stop crying. She realized that Malcolm had been more than her partner; he had also been her lover. She also knew that it was the last time she'd seen him. It was the most horrible experience she'd ever been through, even worse than when she'd been a Union soldier. Much worse. She knew now that the letters tied with red ribbon were letters from Malcolm that she'd kept over the years, after he disappeared in the jungle. She remembered everything about this life... a bad marriage to a doctor after several years of mourning Malcolm. Children. Hiding the letters from her husband in a battered old suitcase in the attic. She remembered her father and his death. He had been the one who built the steps. She remembered every detail about this life, filled with unhappiness. But there was something left unfinished, unresolved... she had died before this thing could be taken care of. This was the only point she wasn't clear on, but she was sure it had something to do with Malcolm and the letters. But the key to the suitcase was beneath the letters inside. She'd have to break the lock somehow.

She awoke exhausted, but burning with the desire to get to those letters. The day passed slowly. She didn't feel like working, didn't really feel like doing anything. As soon as darkness fell, she went to bed. James, always concerned, had asked her what was wrong. She replied that she hadn't slept well, and just needed to get a good night's sleep.

Back in the Violet World, Celeste began climbing the stairs. When she reached the top, there was a hammer and chisel beside the suitcase. A wave of relief swept over her as she began breaking the lock. It didn't take much effort. Inside were the letters, and beneath them not one but two keys. The smaller one was evidently the suitcase key, but the other looked more like a door key. She untied the ribbon from the letters and began to read. They all began "My Dearest Joan". As she read, she *was* Joan. She was overcome with emotion, remembering how much she had loved this man. He'd been a poet besides a medic, and much of what she read were long testaments of his love in poetic form. When she'd finished, she tied them back up and placed them into the suitcase again. The large key went into her pocket.

She knew now that one of the doors was locked, and that she'd need the key when she found the right one.

Each night, she went down the line, trying doorknobs. Each night, she was a different person; different sexes, different ethnicities, sometimes she was even a child. Her fondest one was being a little girl in Jerusalem when she saw Jesus riding a donkey. They were laying palm branches out in his path. She didn't understand what was happening, but she was excited. Her worst one, besides the one in Africa, was in Nazi Germany during World War II. She was a Jewish man in a camp, separated from his family. Once she was a farmer's wife in Russia before the revolution. The work was hard, but they had a large, happy family. Some lives seemed to have been wasted. She lived one life as a spinster who lived to be 94, still a virgin. The common thread throughout all these lives seemed to be that she was always a basically good person. She never lived as a junkie or thief or murderer. That made her happy.

She slowly finished her painting of the Violet World during the day as she explored other worlds at night. Finally, the night she put the finishing touches on the painting and went to bed, it happened. She came to a door that wouldn't open. "This is it," she thought. "This is what I've been waiting for." She slipped the key into the lock.

The door opened into a small café. She was sitting with Malcolm, making plans for the future. They were going to be married, he said, right after the next mission to Africa. This was that one moment in time that determined their future.

"No", she said. "No more missions. We'll get jobs at Saint Anthony's and get married right away."

"But you were so adamant about going just yesterday!"

"This is too important to wait any longer for. Besides, we're both mentally and physically fatigued. We need to get out now, while we still can."

He squeezed her hands with his. "If that's what you want, it's what you shall have."

Celeste/Joan sighed with relief. They'd done it. They'd changed the future. Joan was going to have a happy life with Malcolm and Celeste... Celeste could go back to her life with James. But she couldn't. The door was gone. There was no suitcase full of letters, no key to a locked door anymore. The future had been changed. How could she get back home now?

James knew something was wrong when his wife wouldn't wake up. He called 911 and the EMS team took her to Saint John's Memorial. She'd slipped into a coma. He sat by her bed, holding her hand. All he could think was "Where are you?" All he could feel was misery. After several days, the doctor convinced him to go home and get some rest. "We'll call you the minute anything changes."

At home, he couldn't sleep. Finally, it hit him. He'd taken art in college. He went into her studio and painted a door on her last painting of the Violet World. He painted it open. Taking a couple of Valium, he lay down and waited for sleep.

The Violet World was just as she'd painted it, with the addition of a door at the top of the stairs. James walked up the steps as quickly as he could. The door was open, and he stepped in. Inside Celeste lay in the hospital room, still comatose. Picking her up, he carried her in his arms down all 112 steps. He sat down on the bottom step, willing himself to wake up. The strange music soon became the beeps and blips of a hospital room. He was by her bed, holding her hand, when it moved. Her eyes opened.

"You came for me."

"Damn right, I did, baby. Damn right."

Upon returning home, James took both paintings into the backyard, squirted them with lighter fluid, and watched them burn.

She reflected on all the lives she'd been a part of, and how little her journey had done to help them. But it had helped her. She saw life in a completely new way now.

That night, she lay there holding him for a long time. She was happy just to be where she was for the moment. She swore to herself that they would spend more time together. She knew now just how precious time was.

Mannequin

The wooly sweater was made of thin red, brown and gold yarn. It was on a mannequin in the attic, with empty bird cages, boxes of shoes, old books, magazines, and large containers of winter clothes that no one would wear again. I'd always said that I would clean the attic tomorrow, but that day doesn't exist any longer.

The mannequin wasn't one of those dressmakers' types, but had come from a storefront somewhere. I remember that I wasn't far from home, walking down an alley behind the local strip mall. I was looking for some boxes (I was told later that stores didn't throw away their boxes in big bins as they once had), and there she was. Her white head, neck and a part of her chest leaned awkwardly into the corner of a dumpster which smelled like rotting garbage. Still, I couldn't believe my luck.

"Maggie will find a use for you," I said aloud to no one.

I washed her at the car wash before I brought her home and lovingly presented her to Maggie. And she did like her, just as I had known she would. After all, Maggie loved to make her own clothes for the few special occasions that came our way. But mostly the special occasions came for others who needed Maggie's handiwork. And that's how she spent most of her days, creating fancy clothing for the ones who could afford it.

Maggie could also knit and crochet, and that's what she did in front of the television to watch her "shows". It was the only delight she got out of her day, before she had to stop and cook supper for us. Then, unless it was one of those rare special nights, I'd retire into the garage to work on the Mustang that I was rebuilding, and she would return to her knitting or crocheting.

It was one of those nights, after she had finished a cardigan for her sister, that she leaned in front of her chair and pulled out a rolled ball of brown woolen yarn. Instead of tossing it back into the basket, she began crocheting. After a while she retrieved the red yarn and began to crochet the yarns in an interesting pattern.

"That knitting pattern looks very nice" I said. "Who is it for?"

"I'm crocheting, and it's for my mother. You know how much I hate brown." Maggie didn't pause one bit as she continued the end of the perfectly patterned sweater she was making.

I smiled and bent down low to give her a kiss on the forehead, but she had moved out of the way to get the gold yarn. I stood up, took a look at my wife as she began to add metallic yarn into the beginning of the sweater, then went back into the garage.

My world changed in an instant, forever, when I returned from the garage. I remember Maggie slumped over in her chair, the frantic 911 call, the hospital. I remember how unfeeling the doctor seemed when he told me she was gone. I remember walking through the empty house wailing like a banshee, even though I hadn't cried since I was a child. I remember people bringing food, because I'd forget to eat. Lastly, I remember fighting with a relative who wanted to take Maggie's things away. "On a cold day in Hell! " I yelled at her. She finally left and never bothered me again. Eventually I put her things in the attic, though, because I was breaking down every time I saw them.

The mannequin, still wearing the wooly brown, red and gold sweater, was the last to go into the attic. I placed her right into the center of everything else. The sweater was all she wore. It looked a little obscene, but that's the way she came, and I knew that's the way she preferred to look. She didn't tell me why. I just knew by the look on her face. I named her Cancer, for her lack of hair.

It had been several months, and I could still feel Maggie on her side of the bed whenever I lay down at the end of a weary day. I would say goodnight as I softly cried into my pillow. The medication that my psychiatrist had prescribed would make me sleep if I wanted to or not, and I hated that. I felt so lost that simple chores would overwhelm me. I'd wander through that big empty house by myself, ironing my own shirts, eating my own cooking, cleaning my own messes. Working on my Mustang no longer interested me. I spent my evenings watching whatever new reality or game show as it played out on the television. And every night I cried into my pillow until the medication took effect.

It was night when the singing started. It was soft and low, but loud enough for me to hear from my bedroom. It came for three nights, just as I was turning on my side, waiting for the pill to take effect. The voice was fresh and clean, reminding me of smooth flowing milk. I found I no longer needed the sleeping pills that the shrink had given me. No pill needed, just that sweet voice.

On the fourth night I decided to find where the singing was coming from. So I waited in the hallway just below the door to the attic. I didn't have to wait long before I heard the soft melodic voice that I'd been hearing for the last three nights. Now, standing below the attic door, the voice was louder, yet it was still as sublime as it always had been.

I slowly pulled down the attic door, walked up the stairs and turned on the lights. There she was in the middle of the room where I had placed her. My appearance in the attic did not stop her singing. Still, she looked at me, and made me smile.

She began singing some of my favorite songs from the seventies and the eighties, even some of the songs that you only hear on the radio when you're driving yourself to work and back. Sometimes she would sing when I was cooking or taking a shower. Even mopping the floor came easier as long as I could hear her voice. I went back to working in the garage on my beloved Mustang. Sometimes I'd go up and sing with her. I couldn't get over how beautiful her voice was, and how much she liked to sing for me.

At some point we began talking, telling each other stories from our respective worlds. She told me of the things she'd seen while standing in the storefront, strange things, things that regular people like myself missed. I guess she thought my stories strange as well, of growing up and moving about on my own. She wanted to be able to do that. To walk, to move through the crowds, to experience life as I knew it.

"All day, every day, I had to stand in a store."

"But you don't feel pain", I said. "You stand on your feet forever and never tire. You're the one who has it good. Believe me, you don't want to know the things I know. Not first-hand, anyway."

"I've never tasted food, or held a baby, or made love. Wouldn't it be worth the small price to have these things?"

"It's not a small price, and you pay constantly."

She looked at me, and I looked at her, then retired to my bedroom as she began to sing.

"If I leave here tomorrow
Would you still remember me?
For I must be traveling on, now,
'Cause there's too many places I've got to see. "

We began to drift apart after that conversation. She was as stubborn as Maggie ever was. I said something stupid, like "I can't risk losing you again."

"Again? Who do you think you're talking to? I'm not your wife. I'm a mannequin that you named Cancer."

Eventually, she stopped singing. I came home from work each night trying to work in the garage, or watching television without seeing it. Life became dreary, but I became used to it. I thought about her, up in the attic, not singing, not happy... but I couldn't risk losing the only thing left of Maggie, that damned mannequin in the wooly sweater.

I stopped going up into the attic years ago now, but I know that she's still there. Covered in dust, I guess, but still there. I won't be here much longer, but unless someone moves her, she'll be there for a hundred years. I think I'll go up and move her to the window, where she can see. She deserves that, at least. Maybe I'll sit with her and watch for a while myself.

Not So Wild About Harry

1

The old brick building had a concrete slab running across the bottom of it, large enough for a man to sit on. This is what Harry was sitting on. Harry wasn't as old as the building, but he didn't miss it by much. You couldn't tell his age unless you got right up in his face. He didn't look that old, with a long bushy beard and shoulder-length hair. He could pass for fifty. Like I said, if you didn't get too close. He was sitting there smoking a cigarette, listening to another old man in a woolen cap talk loudly to himself. He tried to keep busy, but when there was nothing to do you could always find him sitting on that concrete smoking. He stopped anyone who passed and talked to them. He didn't try to talk to the only other old man out there today, though; the guy was having a pretty good conversation with himself.

I'm Donald Blaine, another occupant of this old building for old people. I'm fifty-six, one of the younger residents. They're always trying to get me to go play cards or bingo or some kind of crap, but I keep pretty much to myself. Anyway, this day Harry stopped me as I was walking back from taking out the trash.

"Did you know Miss Emma died?"

"You mean the old lady who was always telling everyone that Jesus loved them?"

"Yeah, that lady. That makes two now in a week."

"That's too bad. I'll miss seeing her around."

"Well, we all gotta go sometime. You and me too."

"Yup. I never thought I'd make it this far."

"Ha! Me either!"

The sound of the ambulance's siren was something that occurred so often I almost didn't pay any attention to it at all. Just a thought in the back of my mind... "Someone's having a bad night. Someone may be leaving an apartment empty." I'd ridden in the back of one three times in the last three years myself, but I'd always made it back. Bad heart and lungs. My health went to hell after my wife died four years ago. I haven't helped it any by smoking and drinking too much. But I'm a writer, you know. It kind of comes with the territory.

Anyway, I finally got away from Harry and made it back up to my third-floor apartment. It was cool and quiet, just the way I like it. I grabbed a Budweiser and popped an ephedrine tablet. Thinking about it, I popped another one. My plan was to work on a story I'd been writing until I was too drunk to see the words, then spend the rest of the night surfing porn. I wouldn't be worth a damn for anything the following day, but that's just a fact that I've become used to. Everyone needs a day off to rest once in a while.

Just about the time the words were getting fuzzy on the screen and I was making a lot of typos, I heard the ambulance. The window was open, so it was even louder than usual. I could hear by the noise in the hall that they were right in front of my door. "Well, I know it's not me, I'm not even good and drunk yet." Then, "Damn! I hope it's not Harry." But I could tell from the sounds through the wall that it was. Harry lives next door. I guess I should have mentioned that. He's one of the few residents I know by name, and the even fewer that I actually like. I stood in my doorway, and when they took him by on a stretcher, all I could think of to say was "Hurry back!" I sincerely hoped that he would. The night had suddenly gone sour on me. I poured half of a Budweiser down the sink and went to bed. I didn't sleep right away, though. I lay there smoking cigarettes and watching 'Seinfeld' on DVD until the Valium kicked in.

A couple of days later, I walked across the street for cigarettes. When I returned, there was Harry, sitting in his usual spot. He stood up when he saw me.

"Good to see you, man! I guess it wasn't anything serious?"

"Nah, I died."

"Huh?"

"Yeah, I'm deader'n a doornail. You're the first one to see me since I've been back. Other people just look right through me, even walk right through me. I'm a ghost, cuz."

"Give me some of whatever it is you're taking!"

"Not shittin' you, man. Somebody screwed up and let me die before it was time. Now I'm just hanging out waiting 'til they're ready for me."

"Until who's ready?"

"'til the ones who'll be taking me to wherever I'm going are ready, that's who. It's like waiting on a damn bus."

"So if anyone sees me talking to you, they'll think I'm nutty as the old guy in the cap?"

"Probably so, Don."

"So what was it like? What's it like now?"

"No pain, no bright light, nothing. It was just like getting up and walking back home, but I left my body behind in the hospital."

"Jesus H Christ!" I reached out to tap him on the shoulder. My knuckles hit brick. Harry laughed like hell.

"Well, if you want to talk, come up to my apartment. I'm not going to stand out here and look like I'm talking to myself."

"Nah, not right now, maybe later. I'm just watching the world go by right now. Noticing little things I never noticed before. It's like I can see... clearer."

"Okay, Harry, stop by if you want to. I never asked you in before because I'm usually busy writing, sleeping, or getting drunk. Never needed any human help with any of those things. But now, you being dead and me being a writer... it might be your last chance to get something off of your mind."

2

Around ten o'clock that night I was getting ready to give it up and go to bed. The words weren't flowing, and it wasn't a drinking night. Suddenly, a pounding on the door; "Dream police! Open up!" Harry.

"I thought you could just walk through walls."

"I can. Just bein' polite."

"Well, thanks. I appreciate it. So, what's up, Harry?"

"Look out of your window. See those two guys down there? I think they're after me, and I don't want to go. Not with them."

There were two figures in black robes and hoods. They looked much like the traditional image of Death, but there were no faces or hands... just darkness wrapped in darkness.

"I don't blame you. Doesn't look like the welcome wagon."

"Damn sure don't! I think I'll just hang out with you up here for a while, if that's okay."

"Uh...sure, Harry. I just hope those things don't come in here after you."

"I don't think they can see too well. I saw them before they saw me, and I just sorta faded into the building."

"Just don't ask me to play cards."

"Nah, I was thinking about what you said earlier. I don't have any family, and nothin' to leave them anyway; but I could tell you what's happened with me over the years. You might find something you could use in there for one of your stories."

I told him to just talk, and I'd take notes. He talked all night. There were some interesting things about him that I didn't know. He married a girl right out of high school. His wife had taken their children and left with another man while he was in Viet Nam. He never married again. He'd been a roadie for a band that almost made it big. He'd been in a biker gang for a while. But mostly, it was an ordinary, rather lonely, life. At dawn, I couldn't keep my eyes open any longer. Harry looked out of the window. "I think I'm safe until tonight. Go ahead and get some sleep."

When I did, I dreamed of being chased by black shadowy things.

The next afternoon I sat outside with Harry, trying to talk with him and not look crazy to passers-by. He was pretty excited about having his story told in a book. I didn't have the heart to tell him that his death was much more interesting than his life had been. Suddenly there was a flash of light, like the sun reflecting off of a car, and Harry was gone. Poof. Just like that. "Goodbye, Harry, I'll miss you." I walked back up to my apartment.

When darkness fell, I had the urge to look out of the window. The two black figures were back; closer now than they'd been the night before. "WTF?" (I think in shorthand sometimes.) They looked up at me at the same time. There was an emptiness inside those robes that was the scariest thing that I'd ever seen. They began walking... no, drifting... towards the building.

I remembered my ex-mother-in-law's parting words many years ago: "I hope demons drag you to hell and eat your face." It was a most discomfiting thought at the moment.

I turned every light in the house on, hoping the brightness would shy them away. I could feel them in the building, gliding down the dimly-lit halls. I could feel their presence outside of my door. How, I don't know, but the strategy with the lights seemed to be working. Whatever these creatures were, they liked the darkness. I sat perfectly still for a few minutes, and the feeling of their presence went away. I lit a cigarette and farted loudly. "Yeah, I've got more of that for you bums!" My shaking betrayed my false bravado.

I heard a loud laugh from behind me. There was Harry, sitting on the sofa. "Almost scared the shit out of you, didn't they?"

I'd never been so happy to see a ghost. "I thought you were gone! To heaven or hell or wherever you were supposed to go."

"Man, the afterlife's civil service is worse than this world's. Spirits are like packages, each has its own unique destination. They can't seem to get anything right. Sent me to the wrong place, some other dude's idea of heaven I guess. A desert island! Who the hell thinks that's paradise?"

"So that's why there are ghosts hanging around for hundreds of years? Just waiting for the UPS man?"

"Pretty much. Anyway, I got them to let me come back here and wait. At least there are people around."

"What about these damn things chasing you... and maybe me too now?"

"They're like the IRS. They want to make you pay your back taxes. Wherever it is that they take you, friend, you don't want to go!"

"Well, at least you learned something while you were gone. Tell you what, Harry, in the morning we should just take off. Go on a road trip."

"Sounds good to me. You mind if I have a beer or two while you're sleeping?"

"Hell, if you can drink in your condition, go for it! See you in the morning."

Early the next day, I packed an overnight bag and grabbed my laptop and phone. Harry was bleary-eyed, and all my beer was gone. "I guess you need to sleep sometimes, too."

"Yeah... don't have to eat or go to the bathroom, but after a twelve-pack of Budweiser a little sleep sounds pretty good. You drive."

"Where you want to head out to?"

"Anywhere but Illinois."

We went to Chicago first and hit the interstate. We stayed on various interstates mostly, through Iowa, Nebraska, Colorado, Utah, and Las Vegas, Nevada. We (I) drove during the day, and at night we'd hole up in a motel with all the lights on. The Black Things never seemed to tire, they were never far behind. You could feel them even when you couldn't see them. After a couple of days, we hit San Diego.

We'd reached the California coast. We were pretty much out of options, and those things seemed ready to follow us around the world if necessary. Harry looked tired. I know I was.

"Well, Don, maybe it's time we parted company. You're gonna end up like me if you don't get some rest. Go home. It's me they're after."

"But I can't just leave you here with those things."

"You don't owe me anything, man. You've already done a lot more than anyone else I know would've done. Go home. Publish my book. I think I'll go for a swim."

I watched him walk down the beach and into the ocean. He seemed to disappear completely by the time the water was waist high. I walked back to the car and began the long drive back. At twilight, I was surprised to feel that presence behind me again. Surprised is putting it mildly. I was shocked. A realization began creeping into my thick skull; they wanted me. The damned things wanted me. It would be completely dark soon, and there was nothing but open road ahead for at least forty miles. I looked in the rearview mirror and saw the two shapes in the distance. I pushed that old car as hard as she'd go until I finally made it to a motel on the outskirts of some little town. I went back to the routine, sleeping at night with all the lights on, driving during the day. It worked, and I made it back home. As soon as I walked in the door, I knew something was wrong. That much dust couldn't have accumulated over the length of a few days. And there were sheets covering some of the furniture. Who'd gotten in and done that? Another one of those slow realizations crawled into my brain. I uncovered my computer and typed up this story. When I finished, I walked outside. I didn't need to open the door. Harry was back, sitting in his usual spot. I joined him.

"Goddamnit, Harry, why didn't you tell me I was dead?"

"It just now happened. Time moves differently over on this side. You'll remember the details eventually. There's a lot of things different about this life. You'll get used to it."

I sat there for a while, morose. "So what about those black things?"

"Yeah, I'm afraid we're gonna to have to keep stayin' outta their way for a while. There's been so many deaths in our area lately, they've got the paperwork all screwed up. We all gotta go sometime, but too many at once confuses the hell outta them."

"I thought they had you when you went into the ocean. What happened?"

"I guess they don't like water. I don't know, but the people in charge don't like us to get too far away. I walked out into the water and next thing I knew, I was sittin' back here."

After an afternoon listening to Harry's stories, I began to think about that desert island he'd been on. It was sounding pretty good.

A Brief Dialogue with the Dead

1

Jacob was dreaming about working again. Since his retirement, it seemed to be all that he ever dreamed of. Usually it was factory or construction work, but sometimes it was strange work that made no sense outside of the realm of sleep. Tonight he was running the light show for a Beatles concert from the keyboard of his computer. It was a fun job. Waking up, his first thought was that he'd have to tell Connie about it. Then he realized that she was gone, and a wave of sadness overtook him. At least he'd finally stopped dreaming about hospitals and convalescent homes. He wished that she'd visit him more often in his dreams. Everyone else who had passed on did, on a regular basis. At fifty-six, he knew far too many dead people. Maybe it was the guilt he felt that kept her from showing up too much. He should have been there that night she died. She asked him to stay, but he was so damned tired. He was coming back in the morning, he'd told her. But morning never came for her. The phone was ringing as soon as he'd walked into the house, telling him to come to the hospital. "Is it bad?" he'd asked. "Yes, it's bad." And it was. After four years, that last longing look she'd given him as he left still haunted him. He arose and switched on the coffeemaker. He always had it ready to go; fumbling around with it in the morning was a pain in the ass. Especially those frequent mornings he woke up at three or four AM.

He took a handful of pills, lit a cigarette, and sat down at his computer. He wasn't supposed to be smoking; his lungs were what had forced his early retirement. "Fuck it," he thought, "everyone has to die of something." He'd almost died soon after Connie. He remembered the heart attack, lying on the floor with an elephant on his chest. He'd almost let himself go then, but had decided he didn't want to go that way. He'd wanted to die, but not so painfully. "Chickenshit," he thought. He'd crawled to the phone and called 911.

He checked his e-mail to see if any of his work had been accepted anywhere. He'd been writing since her death, and was finally gaining a little recognition. At first he'd written hundreds of poems detailing his sorrow. Finally sick of himself, he'd begun writing short stories, trying to use his imagination for something other than dark and dreary poetry. It seemed to be working, at least a little.

Dawn came into the room and put her hand on his shoulder. She'd come after his heart attack and never left. Probably the only reason he wasn't dead now. He told her about his dream, and that he'd had another piece accepted for publication. She was happy for him, and kissed his lips. "A good woman," he thought, "She deserves more than I can give her." He knew that he was generally quiet, even sullen. He couldn't understand why she loved him. For whatever reason, she evidently did. She didn't have to stay, but she stayed with him anyway. He worried about her health. She was two years older than he was, and had a lot of problems. He couldn't allow himself to love her the way he'd loved Connie; he couldn't go through that kind of loss again.

The sun rose and shone brightly through the blinds. It was October, and the leaves outside were changing into beautiful colors. He thought about Connie again, and how much she loved autumn. She'd loved the Cubs, too; he was almost glad that she hadn't been able to see the woeful seasons they'd had since Lou Piniella left. Not that they'd ever had a real championship season in her lifetime. He wondered what the mystique of the Cubs was, why they had fans all over the country when they so often sucked. She'd made him a Cubs fan too, though. "Okay," he told himself, "Let's go to work."

"It was a dark and stormy night," he wrote, smiling. He still had a limited number of smiles left; he tried to ration them. He didn't want to run out.

After hearing about Jacob's publication, Dawn was so proud of him that she decided to cook breakfast. No, Dawn didn't cook breakfast each day, nor lunch. She was a modern woman and figured Jacob could fend for himself some mornings. He liked grits, so she always made sure there were plenty of instant flavored grits in the house. She was good about that, making sure he had the things that he liked so that he could have breakfast or an early lunch. There were times, though, when Jacob would eat leftovers for breakfast. She had to yell at him, "Those leftovers are for dinner!" Those times often found Jacob making a sandwich instead.

That morning, as she was putting the bacon into the pan, Dawn realized that she was feeling well, better then she had for the last few days. She had had flu symptoms, but didn't want to go to the clinic unless it was absolutely necessary. She'd rather "ride it out." She had spent three days in bed eating nothing but Campbell's chicken noodle soup and saltines. On the fourth day, she felt like she finally had the energy to get out of bed. The rest and chicken noodle soup really helped her kick that flu. The oranges, limes and lemons cooked down, and added to a glass of Orange Triple Sec didn't hurt either.

They ate breakfast. Dawn was keeping the conversation going, as she always did, when she announced that she wanted to read the story that was going to be published. It's probably one that she had read already, she thought, but she couldn't remember by the title. She didn't always get around to reading something new when Jacob had finished writing it. Still, even if she had read it before, the story could have grown and changed since she read the first draft. Jacob brought the text up on his monitor screen and got out of his well-worn chair so that she could read.

After just a few sentences, Dawn realized that Connie had once again made her way into his story. At least, it had been a while, but it was the biggest reason why she had not read most of his earliest prose. She didn't want to have that feeling of disloyalty again. She was the one who had encouraged Jacob to write, and she was happy that his writing kept him from going insane, or worse. But that didn't mean she didn't feel her heart tear off a thin layer every time something came up that involved Connie

It was bad enough that there were reminders of Connie throughout their house. The living room furniture that they had bought together, the curio filled with items that had once belonged to her grand-mother and mother, the large wreaths on the wall. And last, but not least, her photo was on the wall of their hallway. Dawn was honestly okay with this. After all, it wasn't her place to decide when Jacob was ready to move forward in the grieving process. She certainly wasn't going to remove any of Connie's things. She knew if she did, Jacob would never forgive her.

Dawn stopped reading the story. She couldn't get to the end. She was getting a headache.

Jacob had been hovering over her left shoulder while she was reading. "Well, what do you think?"

Dawn didn't want to voice what she really thought, so she said a simple, "It's fine," keeping the tone of her voice up beat. She stood up from his chair.

"That's all you have to say, it's 'fine'?"

"Yes. I can see why they liked it." She smiled then moved past him and headed over to the kitchen table to pick up the breakfast dishes.

Jacob sat in his chair and swiveled around so that he could watch her.

"What's wrong?"

"Nothing is wrong, Jacob. I don't know why you think something is wrong. Now, let me be. I have to finish the dishes and put a load of clothes into the washer. I would like to get two loads done today before my nap time. And try not to smoke too much today. Okay? You promised."

After writing half of the morning, Jacob closed Word and deleted it. It was crap, and he knew it. He'd been unable to stay focused. He knew that Dawn was keeping things from him. She could be so damned secretive! He suspected that her recent bout with the "flu" was really depression. She always had too many irons in the fire, and sometimes it caught up with her. Now she was freelancing, writing papers and editing, as well as her visual art. "Damn, woman, you make me tired just watching you," he thought.

He thought about April. That was the month he planned to see what was left of his family for the first time in years. It was also the month that their building was going smoke-free. He pulled out a cigarette, put it back down, and went for an anxiety pill instead. She was right, he was smoking too much. "Goddamned things are more addictive than heroin," he thought. Connie had continued to smoke after being diagnosed with congestive heart failure. He remembered waking up often to find her sitting on the sofa, smoking. Why? Because she was having trouble breathing lying down. They would probably be the death of him too. It wasn't a pretty way to go.

It was Wednesday morning. Jacob was up early again. Mornings were best for him. By early evening, he was tired, in pain, and generally sick of the day. This morning, he had no ideas. He wrote:

The dust is back; how does everything become covered in dust so quickly? The bright light of morning shines through the blinds and reveals all. The mask on the wall, the crow on the cupboard, they see it. Shiny smooth black technology is at war with the Victorian scheme of the room, but it all collects the same dust. Suddenly, music drips from my fingers and flowers bloom like madness. Just as quickly everything has changed back, and the sunlight glints off the chrome of my bicycle. Long stripes of shadow cover the walls. The music is all gone, if it was ever there. I am not well. I can hear the colors of madness cooing like doves, while shark eyes watch hungrily. I thought I heard you smile. I walked for a thousand miles in my dreams last night, through the strangest places. I saw you there. I saw you, but could not have you. C'est la vie. C'est la morte.

"More crap," he thought. "Where's my damned muse?"

Dawn awoke from her medication-induced nap to find Jacob beside her. She was surprised that she did not awake when he climbed in. "Boy, upping the milligrams of my pain pills and the new antidepressant really knocks me out," she thought. She looked up and saw her beautiful black cat curled up near the bottom of the bed. Dawn was happy that Jacob had listened to her, (she had been bugging him for three years), and bought the new king size bed. It left plenty of room for each of them to claim a place and still have plenty of room around them. Often, Fritzie would lean up against one of them to sleep. At least she had stopped jumping over them and walking along Dawn's leg in the middle of the night as she used to do.

Dawn wasn't surprised to see Jacob's back facing her in the bed. He'd been up early. He was up again, typing like a fiend by the time she poured her cup first of coffee. She didn't have a moment to say 'good morning' before some foul language came forth from his mouth. She waited to see if anything else was going to happen.

After waiting a reasonable amount of time, she asked, "Are you okay?"

"No," Jacob said bluntly. "Nothing is ever okay." He brought up a new Word page and began to type as if he was angry at the words.

"Okay, then." "Let me know when you have something for me to read." She kissed him on the top of his head. She swore that he had less hair every day.

End of nap time meant a choice of three things: prepping for dinner, writing or editing a freelance task, or working on her own fantasy book. Lately she had added revamping her short stories to the list. They were good stories that had served their purpose at the time (she won big prizes for two of them). Now she wanted to rewrite them, develop the characters and the events, and put them in a collection; maybe someone would be interested in publishing them.

Dawn pulled the two steaks from the refrigerator and laid them down on a cutting board. Meat tenderizer was added, both sides, and she thoroughly pierced the meat. Something her mother had taught her. Then she sat down. The meat needed to get a little warmer. That was something she learned on the web.

She noticed something on Jacob's screen. "Good", she thought, I'm glad he's not awake yet." Dawn took Jacob's chair and scrolled up the pages to find the beginning of the story. She smiled as she read. This story was clever and humorous, something she knew Jacob could write, but hadn't done so in a very long while. She caught herself actually giggling at one particular part. Then her eyes became wide. She didn't want to believe it, but Connie had worked her way into his head and onto the page again.

At that same moment, she heard Jacob waking up. He liked to do a big roar-like sound, like some sort of beast, when he was stretching after a good nap.

When he exited the room, he could see Dawn waiting for him at the end of the hall. Her arms were crossed and her right foot was tapping. Her eyes, if it was possible, were burning through to the back of his head.

"What did I do now?" he asked as he sat on the end of the couch. He was ready to say, "I'm sorry," and give her a big loving hug and kiss.

Dawn didn't sit. "I don't understand you sometimes," she said with her teacher's voice. "After all of these years, you're still stuck in feeling guilty over not staying with Connie when she died." She stood glaring at him, her eyes starting to eat through the back of his head.

Her voice became more intense. "How many times do I have to say it? There was nothing you could have done. It just happened when it happened, for all you know she wasn't even aware that you weren't there.

Dawn looked at him, shaking her head back and forth. Her voice was a little louder. "And how do you think it affects me? It's been four, fucking, years! You'll never get through the process of grieving if you're stuck in that one stage. Do you know what happens to people who do not grieve naturally? They turn into One—Big—Grouchy—Fuck of a person who no one likes, and I don't know if I can take seeing you like that!"

Dawn felt tears forming in her eyes. "I want my Jacob back." Then she held her hands over her face as she began to cry.

Jacob stood and walked towards her to ask her to forgive him. (for what exactly, he did not know) and give her a loving hug.

"Get away from me!" she shouted, and quickly went past him into their bedroom. She locked the door.

After a good cry, she unlocked the door and turned on the DVD player. She put in 'Beetlejuice'. Even though she'd seen that movie more times than she could count, watching it still gave her comfort.

Jacob didn't know what to do or say. There wasn't much that *could* be said when she became like this. He put the steaks back into the refrigerator… she probably wouldn't cook tonight. He knew that she was in pain, and wished that he could change it. Maybe she'd be okay by morning. He was so tired and in so much pain himself, both physically and mentally, that he just couldn't think about it now. "We'll see what it looks like in the morning," he thought.

It was only seven-thirty, but he'd already had enough of the day. His back was killing him, and he could feel a migraine just waiting to happen. Had he taken any pain pills yet? He took some anyway, along with all the others he took before bedtime each night. A valium to top it off and he'd soon be in Sleepy-Land. He thought about dinner. "Screw it; if she cooks I'll have it for breakfast." It seemed that nothing could keep him happy for long. He went to bed without saying goodnight, and was soon in a deep sleep. A very deep sleep.

This time Dawn did feel Jacob come to bed. She had already set herself way on the edge on her side with her back towards him. She was pretending to sleep, but she couldn't. Her "sleepy time" pills were in the kitchen, and she would have had to pass through the living room to get to them.

84

She continued to lie in bed singing songs in her head, especially from old vinyls that she had bought when they were originally released. She slowly remembered the groups and soloists that she loved to download and store in her IPod. So there she was, singing songs by Neil Young from "Harvest" in her head.

Dawn knew that she had waited long enough, that he should be in Sleepy-Land by then, so she slowly got out of bed. She was hungry, but she just grabbed two slices of multi-grain bread, slapped some Miracle Whip on each slice, and stuck a slice of American cheese in between. While she was stuffing that into her mouth, she poured herself a glass of water from the fridge and took her medication down from the cabinet where they each kept their medication. Finish stuffing face, drink a little bit of water, take the meds, and drink the rest of the water. She waited to see if she had to go to bathroom, but that feeling wasn't there yet. She hoped it waited until time to get up.

She returned to the bedroom wondering what would happen tomorrow morning. What would he say, how would she react? She had no idea. Dawn rarely yelled, and only cursed if she was really angry. That should show Jacob that she was serious. She just had no idea how he would react.

She was sitting on the bed, thinking, when she realized that something wasn't right. Something, in the room, about the room, but what? She looked over her shoulder at Jacob, and it hit her. He wasn't snoring!

"Jacob," She shook him, but he didn't stir. "JA-COB!" she yelled, shaking him harder over and over. "Please wake up! Please!"

She grabbed the cell phone on his night stand and dialed 911. "Hurry! My husband's not breathing!"

The staff at the hospital told Dawn that she could not see him in the emergency room, but they'd be moving him into ICU soon. She was lead to the family waiting room. All she could do then was wait. A tall man in scrubs and a white lab coat appeared in the doorway and called her name. She was excited to hear good news; Jacob was alive.

He had come into the room with a woman in a business suit close behind him. The woman was holding a clipboard to her chest as if someone might want to take it away from her. .

He introduced himself as the doctor on call in the emergency room. And he introduced the woman, but didn't include why she was there.

"Does Mr. Ramone keep a list of his current medications?"

"Yes!" Dawn said immediately. She fumbled in her large purse and produced one.

The doctor looked over the medication list with a straight face. "Just a minute." He turned his back on her to have a conference with the woman.

"Ms. Tate, we found high doses of hydrocodone in his system. We pumped his stomach as soon as he arrived, but I'm afraid there were some complications. I'm sorry to tell you, Ms. Tate, but he is in coma."

The doctor continued saying something, but all she heard was "Jacob was in a coma."

Then without realizing that she had sat down on the couch, Dawn was with the woman, who was asking her questions. She heard her own voice giving out words without really paying attention to the questions.

"Yes, he has been sullen, and he is sleeping a lot. But he's been diagnosed as having major depression. I've known him for over ten years, and though he's had some bouts of depression, it's not every day. In fact, these last few days he's been writing, and that always gives him a boost of energy."

The woman was writing something down on her clipboard.

"Wait a minute. You're not trying to imply that Jacob took the extra hydrocodone on purpose?"

"We just need to know any reason why he might have taken an overdose of the hydrocodone."

"No!" Dawn stood up. "There is no way that he would want to die like that! Absolutely not! I don't believe what you're saying; I don't believe it at all!"

After frightening a few people, she left the room just as a little nurse's aide was trying to go in.

"Ms. Tate?"

"Yes. What do you want? I need to go get some fresh air."

"Mr. Ramone is settled in his room in the ICU ward now. You can see him now if you like. It's room number 212."

Jacob woke up at 3:30 am again with the need to empty his bladder. "Wonderful," he thought, "I'll be awake for good now." As soon as he stepped out of bed, he realized that something was wrong. Instead of a wall next to the bed, there were French doors. Everything was reversed. Down the hall he could see the glow of the tiny orange lights on the wreath Connie had made. But they had burned out long ago, and the wreath was in the living room now. It hadn't been this way since... since he and Connie had lived in the old apartment on Church Street!

There was no chance that this was a dream. He knew the difference between dreams and reality. He *was* back at the old place, in the bedroom that he and Connie had shared. Everything was as it had been so long ago. He went to the bathroom without daring to look on the other side of the bed. When he saw his face in the mirror, he was shocked again. He had more hair, and the lines on his face were gone. And he was nude... he hadn't slept nude in years!

He went to the living room, confused but happy. There on the sofa sat Connie, smoking a cigarette. She looked healthy and happy.

"Hey. Couldn't sleep either?"

He was speechless.

"What's wrong, sweet baby?"

"How... what... you're alive!"

"Yeah. I guessed you might wonder about that. We're on the other side of the river."

"I don't understand."

"You've crossed over to where I am. I thought you'd never come."

He pulled her up from the sofa and wrapped her in his arms.

"I'm dead?"

"No, not technically. But you're in a state where you can see me now."

They sat down and just looked at each other for a moment.

"Baby, you know what's been on my mind for so long. Why didn't you tell me that night that you were dying? You know I wouldn't have left if you'd just told me,"

"I couldn't bear to see you so upset. I knew that I didn't have long, but I was hoping like you that it wouldn't be before I saw you again. I saw you that night in the morgue. I saw you kiss me, heard you howl like a wounded animal. Don't worry, sweet baby, I know that you love me. I know that you didn't leave me alone on purpose."

"Even hearing it from you, I can't forgive myself."

"It wouldn't have made any difference. You know how I kept nodding out? It was just like that. I went to sleep and didn't wake back up. You wouldn't even have known."

"But I can stay here with you now?"

"No, you'll have to go back eventually."

"Baby, it would kill me to have to leave you again."

"Dawn needs you now. I'll be here. I just want you to know that I still love you. I'm not mad, or jealous. Dawn has been good for you since I left. You have to keep living. Stop trying to kill yourself... we all end up here when it's our time.

Jacob walked to the window and pulled the curtain. Everything was the same as it had always been, but the moon was a bright white. He felt warm when he heard a shout from across the street; the halfway-house. They never stopped. He smiled.

"What a beautiful life we had together."

"Do something for me, sweet baby. Try to give Dawn the kind of memories you have of us."

He wanted to turn around and take her in his arms again, but the moon was shining ever brighter, ever larger. Everything else was fading away at the insistence of the moon. He opened his eyes to the bright light of a hospital room.

The first thing that he saw was Dawn, sitting by his bed. He managed a weak smile.

She wanted to scream for joy, but she contained herself. "Oh, Jacob, you're back! You're back!" She squeezed his had that she had been holding. "You're back. I can't believe it." Tears started to form at the corners of her eyes.

"What the hell happened?" His voice was barely a whisper.

"You accidentally overdosed on your pain meds. You were in a coma for six hours!"

"And you've been here the whole time?"

A tear left the eye and started rolling down her face. "Of course. I love you, you relentless chore of a man." She smiled.

"I love you too, you silly woman."

He coughed. It was clear, but not hard or very loud. Still, Dawn started to press the call button, but Jacob indicated that he was alright.

"I want to tell you something… don't get mad until you hear me out."

"Hmmm… we'll see." She teased, giving his hand another squeeze.

"I saw Connie."

Celeste's expression changed to a frown.

"No, listen. She told me to be better to you. She's not mad or jealous of you. She says that she appreciates you taking care of me, and that I should do the same for you."

Another tear fell down her face, making her pull a tissue from the box on his tray. She wiped her face and nose.

"You *saw* Connie?" She was finally able to ask, "And she told you that? Where… how did you see her?"

"It doesn't matter. It was while I was comatose, I guess. It didn't seem like a dream at all, though; it seemed really, really real." He coughed again, and this time Dawn poured him a cup of water.

"Take it easy, Jacob. You just woke from a coma. It wasn't a long one, but still..." she said as she waited for him to finish his drink of water. She sat quietly before she responded to what he had said.

She took a deep breath and let it out. "It's hard for me to believe that she said that. She never liked me."

"Maybe you see things more clearly when you're not in the midst of them. She seemed happy. And she emphasized that I should be better to you. I'm going to really try, Dawn. I am."

She bent over and kissed him on the forehead.

"It's okay, but it makes me feel good that you're ready to move forward. That's all I can ask."

"Don't be jealous of the dead, baby; they're not jealous of you."

About a Man

1

"Let me tell you a little about myself," he spoke, taking a long drag on his cigarette. "You may not believe it, but I'm a passionate man. I don't show it much, it's true. But I still love every woman I've ever loved."

He looked at me, reading my face. "I love people. All kinds of people. I understand their problems, I empathize. I'm just not very good at showing it. Oh, I tried. When I was very young. It was too much, too powerful. People were afraid of so much love, such deep feeling. So I learned to hide it. Learned so well that I forgot how to show it. I guess it would still scare the hell out of most people if I let that beast out of its cage. Love. Much talked about, written about, sung about. But how many people even know what it is?"

I didn't have an answer handy. After a minute, he went on. "I've never truly hated anyone. Never had anyone do anything to me that I haven't forgiven. I don't hold grudges. Takes up to much room in your soul; hate, resentment, bitterness. Not healthy. It's like a cancer. Some people let it eat away at them, 'til they can't enjoy the present for worrying about past indignities that the other guy has probably long forgotten."

I was still just looking and listening. I was pretty amazed by his words, having known him all my life and never had any idea that he had thoughts like these. He'd always been likeable, but cold, someone you couldn't get too close to. Maybe he was mellowing with age. He was getting that grizzled look that comes with age. Lines on the face, grey in the beard… how old was he? I wondered.

"The only worthwhile thing in life is love. I'm not talking about storybook romance or bumping around in the backseat. I mean real love. Love has a long memory for the good things and a short one for the bad. Love forgives and forgets. My first wife remembers the problems we had, my faults. I remember her delivering papers with me, her hair in Pipi Longstockings pigtails, wrapped in a serape against the cold night air. That's what I remember."

I nodded, thinking about my own first love. There were some sweet memories there, for sure.

"Love tolerates faults and mistakes. It forgives and forgets. Well, it should, anyway. I know my wife loved me because later she hated me so passionately. The opposite of love isn't hate, it's indifference. You know, I never did say anything bad about her to the kids, even when I was pretty damned upset about her actions. I know that wasn't true in her case, because later they told me. But that was, luckily, after they'd had the chance to get to know me and see for themselves. I was really lucky to get to raise them from the time they were nine and eleven. Maybe I didn't think so once they hit their teens, but I never thought of sending them back."

He paused another moment, seeming to look somewhere in the distance that only he could see.

"I don't see them much anymore. The oldest seems happy enough, though. The youngest... he's in prison again. There's an anger in that boy that I wish to god I knew the cause of. Something happened. Maybe with one of the ex's boyfriends. Maybe that's why she was willing to let them come live with me. I don't know. I tried sending him to counselors, shrinks... didn't help. I kept hoping he'd grow out of it. But anyway, they both remind me of myself. The older one responsible and centered, the younger full of rage and disappointment. Two sides of me that I've had to try to reconcile all of my life. They each just got more of one part. Smart boys, though. I bred well. My family's curse was having a smart mind for book learning but not a damned lick of common sense. Well, at least the men. The ex's family was strong on good common sense and work ethics. My boys got the best of both sides in that deal."

"I don't think I ever met your sons," I said.

"No, probably not. I moved up here after my accident, and that was several years after they were grown and gone. Anyway, I'm damned proud of 'em."

He stopped and lit another cigarette, coughing. "These damned things are going to kill me."

He looked at the cigarette in his hand like it was an alien stool specimen. "I quit for a year once. Last time I only made it a week. It's because I like the things too much. It's easy to stop doing something you don't like, right?"

I nodded.

"Yeah. Damn right it is. I tell you though; three of the best things I've found in this life are sex, beer, and cigarettes. The bitch is that the last two can interfere with the first. Three goddamn things to enjoy and two

93

of them fuck up the other. A cigarette sure compliments a beer, though."

I nodded again.

"You have no fucking idea, do you? You ever smoke or drink? Hell, you ever get laid?"

This was the man that I was used to. I wondered how many beers he'd had. Maybe this was the end of the sensitive stretch.

"Sure I get laid. Plenty. I've drank some, too, just never liked it." I replied.

"You'd have liked it better with a cigarette."

2

It was six months before I saw him again. He looked a little thinner, a bit more haggard, but still full of pepper. We sat in the park on a bench, me throwing breadcrumbs to the eager ducks and birds, him drinking from a paper bag.

"Well, you getting' any?" he asked.

I nodded affirmatively, only a little embarrassed.

"Good" he said. "Men get weird when they're not gettin' it. That's what makes all these people want to fight. If they were getting laid, they'd be too content to have wars."

"Yeah, I guess you have a point. I'm pretty damned happy," I smiled.

He smiled back. "Yeah... the best thing ever invented. You know I split up with Shelley a couple of months ago. Not getting' as much as I used to, but I'm not able to get it that much anymore anyway. You know a funny thing? When a man's got a woman, all the other women want him. Then, when he becomes available, they're nowhere to be found."

I nodded in agreement again. "Yeah, that does seem to be the way. Sorry to hear about you and Shelley. You've been with her a long time, haven't you?"

"Yeah. Nothing lasts forever. Hell, even if you stay with someone 'til one of you dies, one still ends up leaving."

"Mind if I ask what happened?"

"I don't mind you asking, if you don't mind me tellin' you it's none of your business," he smiled wryly.

"Sorry."

"Hell, don't be sorry. Never know anything if you don't ask."

"Hey kid, you ever think about dying? About what it'll be like, how you're gonna go, what there might be after?"

"Nossir, I don't think much about things like that. I guess I have some, when I used to go to church. But not much."

"Well, you're young to be thinking about such things. When you get older, you start to wonder. I figure I'm ready. Not that I'm in a hurry, but I figure I'm ready to go when my time comes. Be interesting to find out if there's anything over that horizon."

"You're going to live to be a hundred," I smiled. "You're too ornery to die."

He chuckled and coughed. "You're probably right about that, probably right… if there's such a thing as heaven and hell, they're probably flipping a coin to see who has to take me."

His cough sounded worse than it had six months ago, it rattled in his chest.

"When's the last time you saw a doctor?" I asked.

"When's the last time you changed your drawers?"

I took that as a "mind your own business" and shut up about it. We sat in silence for a while, the sounds of the birds and children's laughter and all the other sounds of a late April day swirling around us. I looked at his face and caught a look of extreme sadness pass over it like a cloud. Deep in thought, he seemed to have forgotten that I was even there.

Suddenly, he turned to me and spoke. "I miss 'em, you know. Not just Shelley. Every damned woman I've ever loved. All different, but all with their own lovable qualities. The meanest woman I ever knew had good qualities deep inside. I don't think I've ever met a truly bad person."

"You didn't know my algebra teacher."

3

"Get that sonuvabitch outta here!" I could hear him yelling from a distance down the long clinically clean hall. I knew which room was his when I saw the padre beating a hasty retreat out of one of the doors. He passed me looking straight ahead, a strange, pained expression on his face. I couldn't help but smile. The Old Man never was much on organized religion, and wasn't changing his view now just because he was sick. His scowl brightened when he saw me.

"Hey, kid! Got a cigarette?"

"You know you can't smoke in here."

"Who can't? I'm paying the bills here, or at least the insurance company is."

"It's against the rules, and for a reason. Look at the oxygen tanks in this room! Besides the fact that you don't have enough lung left to suck in the smoke."

"Smart-ass kids. Rules, regulations, snot-nosed kids running the world, acting like they know something…"

A spasm of coughing broke him off there. It was so bad that I was about to push the buzzer for a nurse when he finally began to stop, taking in short pained gasps of air. He put the oxygen mask on and closed his eyes.

"I would ask how you've been, but you look like crap and sound worse."

He was still getting his breathing back to normal, so I told him a little about what had been going on in my life. I was careful not to say anything to upset him.

Finally, he spoke.

"Boy, you've had a whole lot of blah since I saw you last. Thought you'd have married that girl by now, had a kid. At least one in the oven. You got your degree, right? Well, maybe it's for the best. You should take some time for yourself, see a little of the world. Get it out of your system, so you won't start wondering what you mighta missed five or ten years down the road."

"Yeah, I will. Don't worry about me. You need to take care of yourself."

"Boy, I'm dyin', and that's that. I'm not coming out this time, they told me. They might move me to a nursing home if I don't die quick enough."

"Jesus."

"Jesus ain't got nothin' to do with it. I don't know what happens when you die, if anything. But the last thing I expect to see is a carpenter from Nazareth. Hell, I couldn't get a plumber from the city out to the house last year!"

"I don't know what to say..."

"Nothing to be said. You live your life to the best of your ability and die dissatisfied. There are always things you could've done differently, wished you'd done better. You just have to realize your limitations and don't waste a lot of time with regrets. If you feel like you did the best you could, dying's not so bad. Especially when your body's in revolt, and doctors and medicine start to be the biggest part of your life.

I was at a loss. What do you say? Been nice knowing you? What I said was "You've taught me a lot about life over the years. I wish I'd spent more time listening to you and less screwing up. I'm going to miss you."

He didn't yell, but said rather gently "Well listen to what I just said about regret. A waste of time, the past can't be changed. Be glad for what you've had, and for what you will have in the future. Don't be too hard on yourself. The human race is really just a bunch of fuck-ups. It's our nature."

He reached out and grabbed my hand tightly. His eyes closed, he heaved a big sigh, and he was gone. Just like that. I rang for the nurse, and was hustled outside while they tried to resuscitate him. I knew he was gone.

I stood there for a while, feeling numb. Then I almost smiled... hell, maybe I did... at the thought of his last words. Then I cried a little, unexpectedly. Finally, I collected myself and walked out into the bright daylight.

Boys Don't Keep Diaries

(November 10th, 1996)

We were moving from the beautiful home we'd worked so hard to acquire into a small apartment. Health issues, auto accidents, a general string of bad luck. I won't bore you with the details. It was while cleaning out the attic that I found it; a cardboard box filled with composition books. Neatly organized, stored and forgotten for so many years, they contained the sum of my youthful life. I took them down to the nearly empty room that had been my study, sat on the floor, and began to read.

*Feb.08, 1964

I'm starting this diary. Daddy says that boys don't keep diaries, but I don't see why not. Larry has one. Anyway, I think sometimes it would make me feel better if I could just write things down, kind of get them straightened out in my head, you know? Anyway...

My name is Robby Gray, and I'm nine years old. I love reading, drawing, and the Beatles. School is OK, but arithmetic makes my stomach hurt. I'm going to be a scientist, archaeologist, or a pop star when I grow up. I have a younger brother Dewey and even younger sister Shelley, a mother and father, and a dog named Ringo. After the Beatles' drummer, you know? He has those same kind of sad eyes. My friend Larry is the only other boy I know like me. The other kids are good at sports and junk, but we don't really like sports. Larry's going to teach me to play the piano. I like staying over at his house. It's quiet and really nice; they have carpet on the floor. His mother says things in French. He has two sisters, but they don't bother us. Funny thing, they almost never have the TV on. My house is always crowded and noisy, and we have wood and linoleum floors.

*Feb.10th, 1964

We went to my grandparent's house today. Not the good ones, but my father's parents. Aunt Odessa lives with them. She's all sour and kind of scary. I heard that she had married a Holiness preacher a while back, but he left her for another woman. There was a big scandal. She came back home and never left again. Anyway...

Sundays always feel strange to me. All the stores are closed, and everything's real quiet. It makes my stomach feel funny sometimes, like when you dream that you're falling. Even the birds sound weird, like they're echoing.

Sometimes I do feel like I 'm in a dream. I like Grandma's house: it's big and white and old. Victor somebody built it a long time ago. It needs painting. There are big magnolia trees in the front yard, so it's always shady.

Daddy parked the Rambler in the drive, and we walked up onto the front porch and went on in. We passed through the empty "living room" and down the hall. There is a bedroom to the left and right, and at the other end, a staircase on the left. The right door leads into the den. It's always hot and stuffy in there. We had to hug Grandma and Grandpa, as always. They seem to want to be hugged about as much as we want to hug them. Grandpa used to be big and husky, a supervisor at the cotton mill. People were scared of him. I think Daddy and grandma were too. He's getting thin and sick, now, and smells old. Grandma is a thin woman with thin lips. She wears her long gray hair braided in circles around the top of her head. They have a color TV, which is really neat! There wasn't a ball game on today, so I got to watch a movie about Pegasus and a guy with a cloak that made him invisible. Then it went off, and it was hot, and I was bored. I went and sat on the front porch in my uncomfortable Sunday clothes and waited for the visit to be over. Dewey and Shelly were playing with a frog. I wanted to be home, drawing or reading.

Finally...

I made it through another Sunday afternoon. Mama cooked pork chops, corn, black-eyed peas and mashed potatoes. That's my favorite. I wish she knew how to make biscuits like Maw-maw, though. My aunts in Georgia can. She says Maw-maw was older when she was growing up, and didn't have the patience. Her older sisters are from Maw-maw's first marriage. That was back in horse-and-buggy days. Pawpaw is Mama and her brother Doug's father. He's tall and funny, retired from the railroad. He used to sing us songs when we were little. "Animal Fair", "Swing Low Sweet Chariot", some other funny songs that I can't remember right now. He's tired a lot now, though, and don't sing much anymore. He still tells good ghost stories when he feels good. Uncle Doug's a greaser. He has a cool car and hangs out at the

Hub and drinks beer. He works for the railroad, too. I'll be glad when summer comes. I can stay with them a whole week! They live in Hamlet. Nobody bothers

me there 'cause it's long distance to call. Gotta go again right now, though; have to study the multiplication tables.I HATE multiplication! We'll have a test on it tomorrow...my stomach hurts...

Feb 11, 1964

Snead's Grove School is a few miles past the cotton mill and church. I ride the bus every morning, a deviled-ham sandwich in a paper bag for lunch. Laurel Hill School is for all the grades except 3rd and 4th. Snead's Grove used to be a high school, too, but it's old now. Daddy used to go to school here. I always look to see if I can find his name carved in any of the desks. It would say "H.W." His real name is Bobby, but he don't like it. Everybody

calls him HW or Mr. H except Mama. She calls him Bobby. They don't have a cafeteria, that's why we bring our lunch. They have a cand candy machine though! When the older kids told us about it last year I didn't believe them, but it's true! I like the Full Dinner candy bars. It's a big square school, with huge oaks and china-berry trees. The walls are cracked plaster, painted pale green. The auditorium is where you walk in, with the classrooms on each side.

Mr. Wright is principal. Everyone's kinda scared of him, 'cause he has a big wooden paddle. We don't have a fire alarm. When we have a drill, Mr. Wright walks around the outside of the classrooms hooting. Miz Pipkin is my teacher. She's pretty nice. I just hope I don't get Miz Reagan next year! I always make As and Bs. C means average, and I don't want to be average. Larry asked if I could go home with him after school Friday and spend the night. I hope I can. Saturday we'll go to Hamlet, and Sunday the Beatles are going to be on Ed Sullivan again!

March 10, 1964

Paw-paw died. I came home from school today and mama was sitting on the couch crying. I'd never seen her cry, and I never knew anybody that died except Will Marston. He got hit by a car last year. I didn't know how to feel. I made a stupid joke to make her feel better, but it only made me feel bad. I guess it was wrong. I wanted to cry, but I didn't have any tears. I sat out on the back porch, not feeling anything.

Later, when I was trying to go to sleep, I started thinking about him. I cried a little bit then.

March 14th, 1964

All my aunts from Georgia came up on the train. We got to stay up late and meet them. I like the train station, they have neat comics. They're the only ones who have Marvel. The drugstore has Classics Illustrated, which are pretty good too. Everybody else just has DC. They had a funeral, but I didn't have to go. I was glad. Somebody took pictures of him in his coffin. They put his glasses on in some, off in others. It was kinda creepy.

June 16, 1964

It snowed on Paw-Paw's birthday. I heard Mama and Daddy talking last night. I think we don't have enough money. Mama used to sing around the house, but she don't anymore. Daddy's gotten meaner, too. I wanted to let my hair grow out like John Lennon's, but he made me go to the barbershop. I don't much like the barbershop anyway. The barber's name is Red, and the other's Bill. He's got a tattoo and smokes cigars. All the men there always think I'm funny for some reason. Red asks me some dumb question, and they all laugh.

Daddy never says anything, he just laughs along with them. He don't laugh at home. I don't know why he stays mad all the time. I wish I could live somewhere else. Uncle Doug moved to Atlanta, so there's nobody left in Hamlet now but Maw-maw. I'm still going to stay with her next week.

June21. 1964

Maw-maw spit a wad of snuff into the empty Peach-Snuff can. "Maw-maw, why am I different than other boys? "What do you mean, different?" "Well, me and Larry aren't good at sports; we're just different from the other kids." "You're not different, you're just like everybody else!" She had a funny look on her face, so I didn't ask her anymore. I think she thought I might be a queer. I'm not sure exactly what that is, but I heard some of the older kids in the boy scouts say it. I don't think it's good, I know that! Did I tell you that Daddy

was the scoutmaster now? Me and Dewey aren't old enough to be boy scouts, but he takes us to the meetings, anyway. The older kids pick on us, especially me. Dewey can fight, but not kids that big. I don't like fighting.

Shelley doesn't have to fight. She's a girl, and the baby. She don't get picked on by anybody, even Mama and Daddy. I guess she don't give anybody any trouble. She's always nice and happy. Well, Dewey picks on her. I do too, sometimes; I guess because hardly anybody else does. She tattles when we do something we're not supposed to. Me and Dewey would still fight anybody that tried to pick on her.

September 2, 1964

I got Miz Reagan.

December 17, 1964

I was a shepherd in the church Christmas pageant. I had a big scab on my head from where I fell off of my bike. My stomach hurt, too. But, Christmas is only 10 days away! It's starting to feel like Christmas now, with the specials on TV and everything. It's my favorite time of the year. We got an aluminum Christmas tree with a color wheel that makes it change colors. Shelley still believes in Santa Clause, and I think Dewey really does, too. He says he don't, but I can tell he hopes he's wrong. That's how I was a couple of years ago.

December 26, 1964

This was the worst Christmas. It didn't snow, it didn't even get cold. We didn't get hardly any toys. I could tell that mama and daddy felt bad about it. That made me feel even worse. I know they don't have much money, but somehow at Christmas everything is supposed to work out. "You're old enough to understand, Robbie." No I'm not! I'm tired of everybody thinking that I can always understand, that I'm so smart, that they expect more from me because my IQ is high. I just want to be a normal kid in a normal house! My nerves are getting worse; I feel weird around people I don't know. My friends in school are the smart ones, but I feel dumb around them. I wish I could go live with Maw-Maw, and never have to go to school.

I haven't written in this journal for a long time. I guess it's because nothing much has happened. I had another birthday. Everything's just been boring. School will be out soon, so I'm getting excited about that. Until summer, Saturday's the only good day in the week. Sundays it's still church and Grandma's. At least we get to go to the plain church. There are two Presbyterian churches here, a big fancy one and a small white wood one. All of my aunts and uncles and cousins go to this one. The same preacher, Tom Young, preaches first at our church and then goes to the other one to preach. Ours is called Ida Mill Chapel. It doesn't matter as much what you wear here, people just wear the best they have. Some of the old people wear overalls. I still have to wear dress pants and a tie. The pants feel itchy and the tie bothers my neck. When I grow up I'm never going to dress up or go to church. Grandpa's getting worse off. He can't go to the bathroom anymore. When he has to go, we leave the room and they bring him a pot. When we come back in, it smells like old man poop. He's going to die soon.

*April 10th, 1966

It was another bad day today. I didn't get into the Beta club. I know all my friends did. I guess I haven't worked as hard this year. Things just bother me, and I don't care as much about schoolwork. I feel like I want to go home, but I'm already here.

*May13th, 1966

Me and Dewey and Andy got some cigarettes! Daddy asks me sometimes to walk to the store and get him a pack of cigarettes. I just went and bought them like I was getting them for him. Had to get Camels, though, or the Marshalls who run the store would know and tell Daddy I was up here trying to buy cigarettes. We went out behind Andy's garage and smoked some. They made us cough, but we smoked them anyway. I had snuck one

now and then from Daddy, but we never had a whole pack before. Mama smokes Salems. They have filters, but they're menthol. They're for girls. Andy's going to try to sneak a beer from his daddy next. Mine don't drink.

I've been hanging out with some of the other kids. They're a lot groovier than the brains. I don't even see Larry much anymore except in class. Jerry lives with his Grandmother. She's old, and don't know what's going on. He can do just about anything he pleases. He stays out at night, and thumbs to Haleyville and sneaks into the movie theatre. I wish I could, but my house is so small Daddy could hear the door creak or the window raised. I can't fart in this house without somebody smelling it. I know...I can tell them I'm going to stay with Larry, and then go to Jerry's! Yeah!

May20th, 1966

We got the beer. I thought Andy was playing a joke on us and had peed in the beer can. That's how bad it was! How do people LIKE this junk? We just had the one can between the three of us, and I was glad. Any more and I'd have been sick! Still, I did get a little happy feeling from it. Maybe we can get something besides Blue Ribbon next time.

July 14th, 1966

All the talk lately's about the niggers marching. Martin Luther King has them all stirred up, and they want civil rights. Whatever that means. I don't really understand it all. I don't know any, except Rob who picks up the trash, and his wife Alameda, who used to baby-sit for us. They have their own section of town, their own stores and houses. It looks nasty, but I never thought about it much. I guess they're the only ones poorer than the whites in my part of town. Oh, and the whites in Bayfield. They're only half a step above the niggers. I guess we're a whole step. Anyway, Daddy says we have to stop calling them niggers and say Negro or colored people. He don't much like it, but I guess he's going along with it. I have some uncles that they say are in the Klan. I don't even want to hear what they say, they're ignorant. I don't know why people would think they're better than somebody else just because they were born a different color. How can you be proud of being white? It's just the way you were born, not something you did yourself.

July 30th, 1966

John Lennon said that the Beatles were more popular than Jesus. I saw on the news where they were burning their records in Alabama in big bonfires. It's not what he said that bothers me so much, but why. I thought they were nice guys. Now that they're rich and famous, their heads have gotten big. I'm not going to listen to them anymore. It almost feels like when Will got killed- kind of an empty spot where something should be.

Aug 5th, 1966

I went to summer camp last week, at Camp Morrison. It was a lot of fun. We went swimming twice a day, made some projects, had bible study. That was all good- Well, except for the bible study- but the really fun thing was the guys in my cabin. They were from bigger towns and cities, and seemed older than me. They cussed and told dirty jokes, especially Norman. Tim, our counselor, kept telling us to get our minds out of the gutter. Even the girls were fun. Maybe they're not so bad after all.

* *Aug.11th, 1967*

What a dummy I was to stop listening to the Beatles! Who cares what John Lennon thinks- I just heard Sergeant Pepper! I'd rather listen to them than some preacher telling me how I'm going to hell. Anyway, I got saved, so that means I can't. I think. It's so funny, some people won't even say Hell, like Maw-maw- she just says "the bad place". I found out that you won't get struck by lightning for cussing or listening to rock music. Or smoking and drinking, for that matter. I never understood why you had to be eighteen and then it was OK to do all this stuff.

…..

I looked up from my reading, and noticed the light was becoming dim in the room. I felt strange; images stuffed away in some dark corner of my mind had been released. I put the notebooks back into the cardboard box and got on with the business of moving, but the feeling remained. It was a month later before I was able to return to the diaries. I noticed that there were some missing between the last one that I'd read and the next. Maybe they'll turn up later, maybe they're gone forever. I guess I'm wondering the same about my old life.

…..

*June 22nd, 1968

The whole world's gone crazy. Vietnam, riots, murders, assassinations. Robert Kennedy and Martin Luther King both dead. I don't think there IS a future. Everything seems so mixed up, so hard to understand. It's almost funny when somebody asks me about future plans. How do you plan for anything when the whole world changes from day to day? I heard someone say "stop the world, I want to get off". I know what he means.

*Nov 7th 1968, 4:09PM

I'm back. Nothing's changed, but everything's changed. We went to Hamlet last Saturday. Daddy had to work, and Mama had to get groceries, so they gave me a $10 bill to go to the barbershop with. I put it in my pocket and just kept walking. I didn't even know that I was going to do it until I passed the barber's. It was the strangest feeling: exciting, scary, surreal. The songs from the radio played over and over in my head, while the birds cawed their own tunes from the trees. God Damn, I felt free! Free, but so suddenly alone. For miles, there was nothing on either side of the road but trees and scrub. I heard a car coming a couple of times, and hid in the brush just in case it was them looking for me. It wasn't. They probably had no idea which road I'd taken. As dusk fell, I realized I'd taken a very lonely and little-used road. The day had been warm for early November, and I hadn't worn a coat. The night quickly became raw and breathtakingly cold. Exhausted, I made a bed of straw beneath one of the tall pines and sank into a restless sleep. Images from every horror movie I'd ever seen, every ghost story I'd ever heard, all began to fill my head. I heard chopping sounds from deep within the woods, stirrings and scufflings... My body was shaking all over, how much from cold and how much from fear, I don't know. I was dreaming, then, about the warmth and safety of Maw-Maw's house, of Janet, of music. Angels or Faeries came to comfort me; little flickering lights of blue, who spoke soothing thoughts into my brain without making sounds. I guess they're responsible for saving my sanity that night. Next morning, the fight had left me. Hungry, tired, sleepy, I began the long walk back home.

I was sure that Mama and Daddy would be too happy that I was back safely to try and punish me, and I was right. I was hoping that it would show Daddy how strongly I felt about my hair, and that he'd reconsider.

I was wrong. It had bought me a week, and I paid with the blisters on my feet.

*(*Second entry, 8:30PM*)

"Delirium." Now I know what it means. There are some words that you just can't really understand until you've experienced them. "Death" is another. No matter how many times someone tries to describe certain things, the only way you'll ever really know is through experience. Nobody even knows about the time I tried to saw through my wrists with a pocketknife, or took an overdose of Vivarin and puked my guts out. I always heard that suicides go straight to hell, so I guess I was a little scared about that. The main thing that's kept me from killing myself is the pain. If I could get enough sleeping pills, and just go to sleep and never wake up...

I don't understand why I have such big feelings. A lot of people don't seem to feel much at all, and others feel within a 'normal' range. Mine are huge and sloppy; they fall out and embarrass me. Mama tells me that all teenagers go through this kind of stuff, but that's hard to believe. Why am I the only one talking about it? I haven't heard any of my friends or classmates discussing anything more complicated than sports or music. OK, sex, but that's a whole 'nother animal, there. Are we supposed to pretend that we don't have all these feelings, or am I the only one who really has them? Am I crazy? Am I anywhere near "normal"? Why did God make me this way? Or is there a god at all? I can think of the questions all day long, it's the answers that no one seems to have. And the biggest one, the one that I ask myself a thousand times a day: "Why was I even born?"

*May 22nd, 1968

We went to the softball game last night. It's Industrial League, Dad's the manager of the Blue Farm Equipment team. They're the worst in the league, but have the most fun. I met the most beautiful girl I've ever seen. Her name is Gloria. She looked like Janis Joplin, kind of. She has a crooked little smile and sleepy eyes. We kept looking at each other, and it was like electricity shooting between us. We finally started talking, and before the seventh inning we were in the bushes behind the little concrete bathroom building. We pulled our jeans down, and I pulled her shirt up. I've never even seen a girl naked before, and she was going to let me DO IT! I was so excited that I couldn't get it in; it wouldn't go all the way up.She was really sweet! She said we didn't have to go all the way, that I could just rub up and down on her. I think I'm in love.

. . . .

That was the last entry that I found. I remembered loving Gloria deeply, seeing her when I could for the next two years. I inhaled deodorant and cooking spray, smoked pot, and fought with my Dad about my hair until I wore him down. I bought a car from my uncle when I was sixteen, and paid for it by working at the cotton mill after school. I discovered LSD. One Spring day, I walked away from it all and hitchhiked north with some friends. Upon returning, I tried to go back to school, but was completely out of place with Dewey's classmates. I quit, married a girl that I barely knew, and began a different chapter of my life. I wish that I'd kept up that damned journal.

Earthies

1

The rain kept up at a steady drizzle. We were in R Sector, flying low in our small hovercraft. It was my second tour on earth, and I wasn't very happy about it. Who would be? A world where it's always dark, usually raining, filled with various groups who all want to kill you... Fadderman rode shotgun, and we scanned the dark streets in silence. The one certainty here, things were never quiet for more than a few minutes. A constant pounding barrage that kept everyone jumpy and on edge.

The barricaded tenements of the Earthies shone wetly in and out of our spotlights. Here and there a brief electric blue glow shone. We still didn't know what they were up to, stockpiling old electronic equipment, monitors, television screens...

Suddenly a bright white flash appeared to starboard. "Space Cowboys!" Fedderman yelled, sounding high-pitched and strange. I swerved and began maneuvering madly. These fuckers were no joke. A direct hit from their oddball weaponry could slice us into twenty-six neat little layers in a second. I could hear their insane laughter, that's how close they were. These were the worst element on the planet. They killed for the pure fun of it, not caring who. Mindless maniacal violence, bloodlust, no rhyme or reason... pure chaos... A sudden blast from below distracted their attention for a moment, and I zipped away as fast as I could manage. Thank Diosperene for the sentinels!

We found ourselves in O Sector... I'd been too busy getting the hell away to notice where I was going. The bizarre barb wired buildings and broken pavement shone beneath red tinted streetlamps. One wall held several dozen Quarpniums, clinging vertically with their little clawish feet. I wasn't worried about them, though. They usually only attacked if something excited them, like a skirmish between a Sentinel and some Earthies. "That's what I hate about this D-forsaken place", I thought. "Never just ONE enemy, always someone or something else all too ready to jump in."

Fadderman sighed. "D, Killian, I'm ready to go home already."

"We made it through before, we'll do it again."

A sharp cracking sound echoed through the reddish night, and suddenly those D little mutants the Earthies kept were swarming around us. Something that looked like a doll's head melded into a steel pipe came gnashing its sharp little teeth against the screen. Another appeared at the hatch, an Earthie baby with hollow black eyes and a burned rubber and wire body, trying desperately to open it with its worm-like little fingers. One of the Earthies inside must have gotten nervous and sent them out to attack. They were more a nuisance than anything else, but we knew that they could attract the attention of the Quarps and the Sentinels, and we could have a major skirmish with no possible good results. I whipped out and left the Muties flying from the craft, the Quarps just beginning to fly off of the wall in a single motion.

"We could've taken them, Killian, Quarps and all."

"I know, Fadderman, but that's not the mission."

"We need a much less conspicuous way to make an entrance if anyone's ever going to find out what's going on down there."

I managed a half-smile. "They just like to watch blue screens without interruption. That's the big secret."

Fadderman nodded. "And use leftover parts to make cute little mutie-toys for their kids."

"…or *from* their kids…"

A spy among the Earthies. It had to be done. But how? The Council had long known this, but the retirement of Congealius left an opening to act quickly. Ommstei was disappointed with the intelligence gathered from the daily hovercraft missions, the fuzzy photos and vivid descriptions of fights. And time, even here, did NOT last forever. The blue glow from over the city seemed stronger, more rooted now. The daily strain had taken its toll on Ommstei's face. The strain of trying to help people while they try to kill you. For the uncountable-ith time, he wondered why. Take a simple thing such as conversation and make it complicated with death, destruction, and insanity. Why? He sighed. It'd been evident throughout their history, he knew that. Was this race really worth attempting to save? The decision had been made to try. But it could be revoked.

The first step was simple, in a complicated way. Get someone close enough to see without being seen. Learn enough to send in a believable imposter. Get back out alive with the information. Yes, very simple he thought, the wrinkles around his mouth and eyes seeming to deepen instantly. Most Oruvians were smooth skinned and wide eyed, at least until very old. Ommstei was not very old.

Dimilus was dropped off over the murky water and swam in. No dry clothes, no method of contact if things went sour. Completely on her own. There could be nothing for the Earthies to use against us if she were caught. A simple sounding mission; Get as close as possible without being noticed, find out what you can, make it back to pick-up point. "Yeah", she thought. "Simple." With a good look at these guys and enough information about them, a mole could be sent in and finally this mission might begin to get somewhere. Dimilus was excited about this opportunity. If successful, she'd be remembered as the one who finally began to break the stalemate. If not...

She kept the wet hood of her dark jacket on her head to prevent her conspicuously hairless head from being detected. As more rain began to mist down, she realized the folly of trying to keep dry anyway. Scattered along the beach were nasty looking little objects. Some shadowy and unrecognizable, along with bone, weed and glass. A soft blue glow shone from over a short hill. Dimilus started towards the light.

A place where shadows hold only more shadows. Where getting to the bottom of one thing only brings more questions, never real answers. Ommstei sighed. Dimilus had been the right choice. If anyone could get close and get out, she could. Still, he felt a void feeling, a certain edge-of-disparity. Dimi WAS his favorite brother's daughter, after all. This mission was dragging on too long, having too many personal affectations. There was a growing number back home who were ready to renounce their heretofore unquestioned support of all life, and suggesting what would have been unthinkable earlier. Either abandon the mission and leave the Earthies to their own devices, or (even more disturbing), destroy the entire planet to be sure that the Oruvian's mercy wouldn't come back later to bite them in the ass.

Dimilus could hear the crackling in the air, the underlying buzz from all around. The battered buildings were dark, but she felt as though a spotlight were shining on her every move. So many dark doorways, so much broken glass, battered concrete, it was impossible to step lightly. Here, an apartment building glowed that distinct blue from the cracks around its barricaded upper windows. She almost smiled as the line from one of their old television programs came to mind… "This must be the place…."

Dimilus climbed the rickety metal fire escape to the top of the building, where the glow was the brightest. She'd never been this close before… no one had. Peering through the cracks in the boarded-up windows, she saw Them. The Earthies, huddled around a large monitor, seemingly enraptured by the blue crackly static. They were eating and drinking strange food, wrapped in paper and in metal cans. They seemed so D harmless. Their conversation wasn't about overthrowing governments or freedom fighting; no, they were talking about Wally and the Beav, Jerry and George, Fred and Lamont; comparing notes and memories of ancient Earthie history. Dimilus could see nothing but blue fuzz on the monitor, but they seemed to be seeing plenty. Jokes about Depends and deodorant. These people seemed like the least harmful organisms on the planet.

Her report back was this: No need for infiltration. The Earthies were not a threat, but threatened. The horrible mutations and insane creatures that roamed their planet were the reason they were so secretive. They themselves were trying to avoid confrontation, and the bluescreens were simply their way of entertaining themselves while they holed up in their barricaded buildings against the night. They might even be friendly if the undesirable elements were routed from their planet.

Fadderman and Killian had an easier mission, now. The Earthies were not a threat; everything else on that horrible planet could be removed and relocated. There were still the Space Cowboys to contend with, but with enough help they'd have them taken out soon. When the mission was accomplished, it was decided not to invite the Earthies into the federation, but to police them quietly so that things wouldn't revert back to the sorry state they'd been in for so long. Let them watch their bluescreens in peace, and maybe one day they'd be ready for reality.

Volunteers

1

Jimbo sat and watched the march of the trees from his window. They weren't really marching, more like sliding along, digging into the ground with their roots. "Yep, things are different these days," he thought. He poured himself a cup of molten lava and contemplated life. Somewhere behind his thoughts he could hear the sound of eggs breaking in the refrigerator. Another mess to clean.

Plug came and sat at the table with him.

"Them trees are gittin' it, ain't they?"

"Yep. Wonder where they're goin'?"

"Dollars to donuts they don't even know theirselves."

"I found another dry fish bed yesterday."

"Yeah, they're all dryin' up. Damned shame. Well, we can't waste time yammerin' about the good ol' days. The Sweet Thangs will be doin' a house check purty soon. I guess we oughta be gittin' into the shelter."

"Not until I've finished my coffee. Damned things can wait."

"Yeah, right. I'd like to see you look one of them things in the faces and say that."

"Screw you, Plug."

He rinsed out his cup and walked down the steps to the shelter anyway.

What they called the Sweet Things were creatures with four faces, two in front and two in back. They were kind of an alien police force, checking the houses each day looking for Wormwood, the Resistance leader. The aliens themselves were called Gourd heads. They didn't like humans, and it didn't take much to get on their bad side. Better not to be around when they came in.

Wormwood was a Gourd Head himself, but had become the leader of the movement to give Earth back to the Earthlings. The Sweet Things in this part of the country weren't too bright. The best and brightest were saved for the urban areas where the Resistance was strong. Out here in the sticks, people just tried to make the best of the situation. Oh, they'd fought at first; their shotguns were like pellet guns to the Gourd

Heads and Sweet Things, a minor annoyance. After a few resistors had been relieved of their skin, sensible people just went with the flow.

Jimbo and Plug soon heard the Sweet Things upstairs, walking around in their heavy boots. The shelter door swung open and one looked down at them, saying something in their garbled language. They sat still; they didn't want to make any sudden movements. Jimbo spoke up.

"Nobody down here but us chickens."

Evidently satisfied, the Sweet Thing turned and left. They had translators to understand all the languages of the Earthlings. A few of these translators had been stolen by the Resistance, but most people had no idea what these things were talking about. Jimbo had made an educated guess.

"Well, Jimbo, we need to git some groceries in the house. How you wanna do it?"

"Let's live dangerous and take the truck to town."

"Allright. Why tha hell not?"

"Just look out for those trees."

The roads were in relatively good shape compared to other parts of the country. Some large potholes and one crater that had to be driven around off-road lay between the men and town. Nothing their pick-up truck with four wheel drive couldn't handle.

Town itself was a little different now. The big chain stores were inhabited by small mom-and-pop operations, each marking off their own space. Some items were hard to come by. Jimbo missed his grits. Fresh produce, meat and eggs were plentiful though; anything that could be grown or raised locally. Gas was still available, although it was so expensive that most people couldn't afford it. There were still jobs for humans. Their alien overlords needed things built or fixed. It wasn't the Armageddon of the Mad Max stories. It was just... inconvenient.

Plug picked off a deer on the way home and bled it out. Electricity was rationed, so they wouldn't be able to put it in the freezer. They cut off some steaks for themselves and stopped by their nearest neighbor's house two miles from their own and gave them the rest of the deer. They had a big family, and were happy to get it.

Just before reaching home they almost lost everything when a tree suddenly moved into their path. Jimbo swerved at the last minute and missed it.

116

"Goddamn moving trees! Where the hell have they got to go?"

That night over the grilled deer steaks, they got serious.

"Plug, this ain't no kinda life we're livin' here. The money'll be gone soon, and then what? Go to work for those alien bastards? We need to git the hell outta here,"

"What, you wanna go join the revolution or sumpthin'?"

"Yeah, maybe. What else are we gonna do?"

"Just leave everything here?"

"There ain't much to leave, Plug. Take the truck and go to the city. Do somethin' productive for a change."

"Which city?"

"We could go up to North Carolina. I hear there's things goin' on in Raleigh."

"What the fuck. Let's do it."

And so it was decided.

The truck got bogged down in a swampy area just north of the South Carolina border. They had a chain, but no tree to attach it to. Eventually another truck spotted them and pulled them out. They began talking with the driver of the truck; it had a sign on the sides saying 'John's Computer Repairs.' They were talking to John. He shook his head when they told him they were on their way to Raleigh.

"You don't want to go up there. Hellzapoppin'. We have our own Resistance movement right here. Follow me back to the house if you really want to help."

They were mildly suspicious of this guy... he had a Scottish accent. Then again, they were in Scotland County, and he had pulled them out of the swamp.

The repair shop was attached to a house where John and his wife lived. The Gourd Heads had taken control of the internet, but there were ways around it. They were surprised to learn that the resistance was much more organized than they'd thought. The second-line internet kept information and planning flowing from city to city.

"Damn! What's this?" Jimbo pointed at a large mass on the screen with arrows pointing to it from different directions.

"We're going to hijack a shipment of blasters. You can kill Gourd Heads and Sweet Things alike with these, as long as you get a head shot. There are supposed to be 50, 000 of them... enough to really make a difference. We want to intercept them here at this point, far away from the women and children. Just in case...

This will be synchronized all over the world. Wherever blasters are being shipped, we're going to take them."

"How many of there are you here? Do you have blasters now to pull this off?"

"Wormwood himself will be leading around fifty men. Fifty-two, if you're in. And yes, we do have a blaster for each man."

"Well, I guess that's what we came for."

"Let's go into the house and have some supper. We'll have to head for the interception point at 2:00 AM this morning."

John's wife was a good cook. It had been a long time since they'd had a meal like that. They rested comfortably until time to go, enjoying the fullness of their bellies.

It was organized chaos. The Gourd Heads and Sweet Things had no clue as to what had been planned, and were caught off guard. The blasters worked in much the same way as a double-barreled shotgun... and all of these Southern men were good shots. The seized blasters were loaded onto forty trucks, each of which set off in a different direction. The revolution was now much better armed, and much more dangerous. Jimbo and Plug let out rebel yells as they pulled away from the site.

"What a hoot!"

"Yesiree, Bob!"

They took the load of blasters in the bed of their truck to John's house. In the repair shop was a trap door in the floor beneath a desk. It led into a well-built bunker beneath the backyard swimming pool. They cached the blasters there for the time being. Twenty aliens dead and 50,000 blasters missing... things were going to get ugly quickly.

Within a week, reports of Gourd Head killings were coming in from cities all over America and the world. They retaliated by killing Earth-Men at random. The search for Wormwood was stepped up; houses and buildings were ransacked. But the aliens had underestimated the Earthling's ingenuity. This was becoming an all-out war, not just a few humans taking potshots here and there. Alien numbers were dwindling; they'd never expected to need that many to crush a meager little planet like Earth. They had a real war on their hands now. They were feeling something that they never thought that they'd feel... the fear of losing.

Jimbo and Plug went on mission after mission, usually led by John. Sometimes Wormwood himself would lead. He was a really nice guy for a Gourd Head. He gained their respect with his fearlessness. Without him, the resistance would probably have never had a chance.

The Alien council met and decided that they had two options; kill all Earthlings, or leave the planet. If they killed everyone, they'd have to try to import beings from other planets to do all the work that was beneath them. Killing that many people and replacing them with less fierce beings would be a long, distasteful job. It could be done, but was it worth it?

Before they could make a decision, the face of Wormwood appeared on every monitor. The rebels had somehow managed to take over the entire network. He was giving a speech on how they should surrender and go home. This world was not for them.

As hated as he was, they knew that they'd been beaten. This small planet wasn't worth any more of their lives. They evacuated in an orderly fashion, leaving Wormwood to lead the planet through its reconstruction. He became the first non-human ever to be elected president. The trees went back to their proper places and stayed there. Jimbo and Plug got good jobs with one of the reconstruction crews and settled down in the little town that they'd stopped in. It seemed a little crowded at first for two men used to living far out in the backwoods, but once they met Martha and Alma it became a lot better. But that's another story...

"YeeeHawww!!"

Five Bells

In the not-too-distant future, earth has been united under one flag; the One World flag, a white circle in the center of a field of black. The World Health Organization is the strongest arm of the government, and personal freedom has been sacrificed for the safety of all.

1

The bell rang three times. That meant that you had fifteen minutes to finish up your work and get to the dining hall for dinner. George 2001 began putting away his tools, along with the other thousand or so inmates. Although he was hungry, the routine of the WHO Emotional Rehabilitation Center was driving him mad. Every day was the same. No deviations were allowed, ever. Every inmate wore the same uniform, had the same haircut, and followed the same schedule. Seven days a week, no variation. Eat, work, sleep. Daily "therapy" sessions after lunch. The inmates were broken up into groups for this. It was the only time they were allowed to speak. Even then, there were cameras everywhere. No one ever said more than "I'm doing fine," or "all is well with me."

He couldn't remember the last time that he'd sat and watched the sun rise, or been out to a bar with his friends. All memory of outside life was being erased by the maddening routine. There were those who found the structure comforting, and were eventually released. Others were driven insane, and sent to Electroshock Therapy. George 2001 tried simply to bear the monotony and stay out of trouble. He hoped that he would be released before he began acting on the thoughts that were increasingly on his mind; doing those types of things would earn you a trip to the Black Box. If that didn't work, off to Electroshock.

He picked up his tray and went through the line. The meals were invariably the same. Breakfast: Eggs, bacon, toast and black coffee. Lunch: Salad with saltines. Dinner: Meatloaf, mashed potatoes with gravy, green beans. Every night, those goddamned green beans. A paper cup with a sleeping tablet to be taken after dinner. Bed at eight. Four bells. Everyone took their pills; there was no reason to stay awake. To lie in bed with your thoughts was torture. Angie popped into his mind enough during the day, at odd times. Not as much now as she used to, but still. He didn't want to forget her. Why was love such a bad thing? Why could you be arrested and imprisoned for something that felt so wonderful? Yes, better to sleep and not think. He took his pill, emptied his tray, and went to his cell. As he waited for sleep, he remembered an old movie that he'd seen, "One Flew over the Cuckoo's Nest." He remembered the ending, and tried to drill it into his mind not to make those same mistakes here.

One day, (maybe a Wednesday, who knew?) something extraordinary happened. At first bell, there was no breakfast. No sign of the cooks or the workers who ladled out the food. The inmates all stood around puzzled for a while, but dutifully began work at the appointed time. There were no guards there to watch over them. The cameras were not moving. They worked anyway until second bell. Once again, the dining hall was empty. The men were all hungry now, and began to talk and mutter amongst themselves. Talking was forbidden, but there was no one to stop them. None had ever realized that there was no one on duty at night. With each man in a cell to himself and no way to escape, the staff simply left each night. There was a button to push in each cell should anyone became ill, which rang the doctor wherever he might be.

Suddenly realizing that there was a great opportunity here, they thronged the gates. Five bells: emergency. The electric fence was still working; several men who reached it first were electrocuted, pushed forward by those behind. It sounded like a dentist's drill at first, then sputtered and sizzled like frying bacon. George 2001 went in the other direction, looking for the controls to the fence. He found them upstairs, and shut them off. Something had happened outside, something to keep the workers from coming in. He wasn't sure just how ready he was to go out and see. Let the impatient go first. If there was one thing he'd learned here, it was patience.

Looking around, he saw hundreds of monitors lining the walls; cameras were trained on every area of the Center, inside and out. Finding the front gate, he was surprised to see that at least half of the inmates were still inside, looking out at something. He'd have to go out himself to see what. There seemed to be some type of blur over the top of the screen. He walked slowly down and out of the door, his thoughts racing like they hadn't in a very long time. The crowd parted to let him walk through and up to the gates. They were just milling about now, mumbling to each other. Reaching his destination, he saw what they had seen. About half a mile away, the world turned into a mass of swirling colors. There was no horizon line, no sense of direction, just this seething mass of incredible colors. It was almost hypnotic. George 2001 turned away from it; it seemed to be attempting to pull him toward it. He felt that if he'd looked much longer, he'd have wanted to go. He had a decision to make. There was that half-mile strip between him and it. He could take a chance and begin walking the strip, or stay there and wait. If it moved forward, there was nothing that he could do in either case. He began walking north-east, in the general direction of home, and Angie.

It was hard not to look at the thing. With each glance, its pull gained strength. It seemed to be a living entity. It loved him; it wanted him to join it. He tried to keep focused on his steps, and the thought that he might be able to find the one who really loved him. "One step, two step, red step, blue step," he thought, and almost laughed out loud. Laughter and happiness were approved by the WHO, but strong emotions such as love and hate were forbidden. He wondered how one could gain true happiness without knowing love? Their reasoning was that love often leads to jealousy and from there to hate. Hate leads to violence and war. He understood their reasoning; it was a logical progression that had almost ended life on Earth thirty years ago. Still, he couldn't turn off his love like a switch. No one could. Thus the Centers were built. The Center that he had been incarcerated in was only for those who had exhibited love. He guessed that the missing men had walked straight into the Thing, being weak with the longing for love. He tried to keep his focused on Angie. Even under these strange circumstances, he felt that a huge burden had been lifted. He would not go insane in the Center. He had a chance for something better, and almost anything was better than that.

After walking a couple of miles, he glanced over and noticed that he'd gone past the perimeters of the thing. He'd named it Bob, just to have something to call it other than the thing. So it did have an end. There was the clear sky, with the sun high shining down on green fields. Just ahead was I-95, the road that would take him home. His pace quickened as he neared the highway. It was easy to thumb a ride now, with no crime. Before reaching it, he noticed that the cars were not moving. Closer still, he could see that most of them looked like they'd been abandoned, some with the doors still open. Almost all were One World standard issue metallic vehicles. They started by voice command of the owner only. George (just plain George now; he could drop the 2001 outside the Center) began walking north by the side of the road. Night was approaching, and he was tired.

After a couple of more miles without seeing a moving car, he settled into the backseat of one of the abandoned ones for the night. He'd start again in the morning. His stomach complained loudly about the lack of sustenance therein. He checked the glove box and found an energy bar. That would have to do.

Just as he was shaking off the night's dreams, he heard a humming sound in the distance. Quickly he got out of the car and stood by the side of the rode. A small metallic blur appeared on the horizon. As it neared, he waved frantically at the car. It slowed, went a few feet ahead of him, then stopped. It had been so long since he'd had a conversation, he practiced what he'd say in his mind. It didn't work. There was so much to say, he blurted out a string of unintelligible jargon.

"Calm down. Take it slowly."

The driver was a dark young man wearing black, his passenger a strawberry-haired young lady also wearing black.

"What the hell are you doing out here?"

George managed to speak.

"Trying to get home. And trying to find out what's happening, what that thing is."

"You and everybody else! Get in."

They sped down the highway, changing lanes often to avoid abandoned cars.

"I'm Paul and this is Glenda. We're on our way up from Palm Bay."

"I'm George. Pleased to meet you. Can you tell me anything about what's going on?"

"I'll tell you what I know. There are two of these things, each about five miles long and ten miles wide. One is brightly colored, the other very dark. They're moving, but very slowly. I see by your uniform that you must have seen the one at the Center. You couldn't have missed it if you were that close. We're heading for Wilmington to find our families."

"Great, so am I. What does the news say about these things?"

"You know the OWN news, how careful they are about saying anything. They're mainly telling people not to panic, but to leave the areas these things have been or are expected to move to. They call them clouds."

"And all the missing people?"

"It seems that those caught sleeping when these clouds formed were just... absorbed. Others have been seen walking right into them. They seem to have some sort of hypnotic power, and some are more susceptible to it than others."

"Yes, I noticed that back at the Center. It had a strong pull to it. I think half the men there walked into it."

They saw six black hovercraft heading in the direction they were coming from. The government was definitely on the scene. George was glad he'd gotten away from the Center. Either they hadn't implanted a tracking device in him, or the authorities didn't have time to worry about him now. Either way, the hovercraft took no notice of them and went on their way.

They spotted more traffic as they approached Wilmington, and the abandoned vehicles disappeared. A very good sign.

"Where is the other cloud, the dark one?"

"New York City."

George quickly realized that the two clouds had formed near two of the largest Centers. The WHO Center in New York was for those with emotional disorders related to hate. The one he'd just left was in Atlanta. What were these damned things? There seemed to be a very simple explanation, but it eluded him at the moment. It would come. George was not an unintelligent man.

The young couple went out of their way to drop George off at Angie's house near the beach. He thanked them profoundly, and gave them his number and address.

"If you ever need anything, call me. I mean it."

They wished him luck and drove away. He went around to the back to wait. She would be at work now, if everything was okay. If she didn't come home… he'd cross that bridge when he came to it. He was too tired and hungry to think any more. He sank into sleep on the patio.

Angie left the office late. She'd been having trouble concentrating, worrying about George in Atlanta. She wondered if he still remembered her, or if they'd already managed to exorcise her from his mind. He was all that she seemed to be able to think about lately. She'd finally given up and put away the blueprints that she was working on for the new mall. There was plenty of time before the deadline. Maybe she'd take tomorrow off and do… something, she wasn't sure what. She felt a strong need for change of some sort. The house seemed so empty now, without him. She replayed the night he'd been taken away as she drove. He had lost control, and let his passion for her be unleashed in their lovemaking. She had held back, tried to warn him… within an hour, he was being taken away. "Damn all these rules!" she thought, stopping at a checkpoint. Who knew what they were looking for this time? She wanted to curse at the guards, but smiled pleasantly instead.

Home, she turned all the lights on, inside and out. It had become a habit lately, using light to stave off the loneliness. She stood at the door and looked out, wanting to explode in anger, but keenly aware of its consequences.

George awoke when the backyard lights were switched on. When he saw her face at the door, it was hard to contain his excitement. She knew him immediately, even with the odd haircut and uniform. When she opened the door, he wanted to sweep her up into his arms and cover her with kisses. Instead, they kissed politely. They didn't want a repeat of the night he was taken away. Those damned sensors were everywhere. As he ate and drank, she told him what she knew of the situation.

"I was so worried when I heard the news about the cloud in Atlanta! All I could think of all day was you. They're not giving out much information about what they think these clouds are, or how they plan to stop them. Just the usual warnings about going into the affected areas, and to stay calm. They promise more information later, but it keeps getting later and they're repeating themselves."

Angie hesitated. "I could try calling John…"

George tried to calm the wave of irritation at the mention of his name. John was a high-level government operative and her former lover. He had always suspected that John had something to do with his incarceration.

"No…only in an extreme situation. I don't trust him."

John sat in his office, rubbing his tired eyes. He'd been staring at his computer for hours. The drones had done their job; the information they'd returned was incredible. At the core of each cloud was a large pale entity that looked like an overgrown maggot. They didn't register as human, animal, vegetable or mineral. They didn't match the profile of any known alien beings. As he sat and thought, a woman popped her head in the door.

"Clouds have formed outside the Emotional Rehab Centers in London, St. Petersburg, and Tokyo. We're sending in drones, but expect that they're all the same."

"Thank you, Ms. Drake."

His calm and polite demeanor did not match the anger and confusion he was feeling. They'd already lost aircraft and men on the ground around these things. The only solution seemed to be to drop bombs down from the top, but they reached too high for normal aircraft to fly over. Countless inmates of the Centers had disappeared. There was no way at present to know how many had escaped and how many had been absorbed. They'd have to worry about that later, though. Right now, something had to be done about the clouds. What at first had seemed like movement had been discovered to be growth. They were expanding. There was a meeting in five minutes. What would he tell them?

"Ladies and gentlemen, the process of evacuating everyone within a thousand mile circumference of these clouds has begun. I suggest that we dust off the old spacecraft and drop smart bombs into the center of each."

Professor Malcolm disagreed.

"We need to know exactly what we're dealing with before taking such drastic measures. It could be that without the energy of the humans surrounding it to feed on, these clouds may shrivel and die on their own."

General Tchaikovsky took the middle road.

"Prepare the bombs, but wait. The Professor is right. We need to know what we're destroying before we do it, if at all possible. We need to know what caused these things to form. We know that they're connected to the Centers, but in what way? Are they alien creatures that feed on emotion, or are they a natural occurrence *caused* by so much pent-up emotion? We need to know. Some radical changes may have to be made, and we're not the ones to make that decision. Keep investigating. I will make my report to the president."

John left the meeting with a sour stomach. He believed in swift action, not endless debate over what the things were. "Kill them first, then analyze them," he thought. He locked his office and went home to sleep for a while. His brain was too tired to think about it anymore. However, his dreams were disturbed; he kept hearing a voice calling to him through a swirling mass of deep purple, blue and black. "*I love you... I need you...*"

George awoke beside a still-sleeping Angie. Giving her a light kiss on the cheek, he got up and switched on the coffee, then the news. By the time he'd had his coffee, he switched the news back off in disgust. He was restless. He needed to go somewhere, do something. But what?

Angie dressed and sat down on the edge of the bed. She could hear the news on in the next room, but wasn't ready yet to join George. Deep in thought, she wondered; wouldn't things be so much easier if she'd married John? She loved George, but what kind of future did they have, supposing there was a future at all? The random sensors could pick up strong expressions of love or hate anywhere in the world. Almost surely John had one trained on her home. He was jealous, although careful not to show it. Sex was allowed, of course, but not passionate sex. She'd never had to worry about that with him.

She called her secretary and told him that she wouldn't be in today. Just as she was thinking of calling her sister, George walked in.

"You're going to have to call John."

"Are you sure?"

"Not at all. But I have an idea. Only the government can get this done. A human-sized pod on the end of a robotic arm could penetrate a cloud and allow a person to explore its core. I'm volunteering."

"George, why do you think this is your responsibility? And what makes you think he won't just have you arrested? What about *us*, George, our future?"

"You haven't been close to one of these things. If you'd seen one, up close... there might not be a future if someone doesn't do something. I think John will be happy to send me in. I know that he'd love to have me out of the way. And I was... *am*... a scientist"

John's reaction was as George had expected. He knew that George was qualified to go in, and secretly hoped that he would not come back out. A failed attempt of this kind might get him the OK on the bombing. And with George dead, maybe Angie would come around. He'd been mistaken thinking that having George locked away would be enough, but if there was no chance of his return...

The pods were already in existence. All he had to do was equip one with the instruments George requested, attach it to the arm, and attach the other end of the arm to something large and heavy. The Center itself would work. He was forced to tell George everything known about the clouds. Within three days, all was ready. They had chosen the one in Atlanta; the one in New York had already enveloped the Center there. Angie took some vacation time and flew down with them, against both of their protests. The tension between the two men was palpable. There was nothing left to discuss about the operation, so they rode in silence. John was seething inside as Angie clasped George's hand. He didn't understand why his hatred was so strong now. He'd always prided himself on keeping his emotions in check. Somewhere in the back of his mind, a dark cloud was roiling. His sleep had been restless lately. There was no time to have himself checked out though; this operation superseded everything.

When they arrived they immediately donned soundproof suits. They would have to communicate by radio from now on. The cloud's pull seemed to affect the aural more than anything else, and it was stronger now than when George was last there. Three hundred inmates had been evacuated. The rest were unaccounted for.

A large crowd of suited people were standing about. The arm had been bolted and welded to the Center and the pod. Everything had been checked several times. There wasn't much activity now. The waiting had begun.

George stepped into the pod and the door was soldered shut. Angie put her hand against the glass, and George placed his against hers from inside. John impatiently gave the order to proceed. The pod slowly moved into the cloud of colors.

Even through the soundproof pod and suit, he could hear a faint singing sound. He felt a vibration, soft and warm and loving. It was difficult to stay focused. He began running equations in his mind to override the sensations. The colors seemed thinner inside; he could see the city, lying in a fog of colors. It was empty and eerie, like a strange dream. He was drifting, drifting... "Snap out of it!" he shouted to himself. The voices on the radio were buzzing bees, hard to understand. Then he heard Angie. Focusing his mind on the sound of her voice, he moved forward. Further in, he spotted it; the huge pale thing, sitting there, moving slightly as though it were *breathing*. He couldn't get any closer, the vibrations were too powerful. It made him want to leave the pod and join it, be one with it. Luckily, there was no way to exit the pod. If he hadn't been sealed in, John would surely have gotten his wish. He fought off the feeling, saying Angie's name over and over in his mind, and trained the laser on the thing. As it cut into it, there was a terrible rumbling. The pod shook as he tried to cut a circular hole. The shaking was so violent, it seemed that the pod might break away from the arm. Slowly he managed to cut a jagged hole in its side, large enough for the pod to go in. Everything was shaking, and the faint singing now sounded like screaming. His mind was becoming clearer. The thing began to deflate slowly, like a balloon. As it did, bodies began floating out of the hole that he'd cut. He couldn't tell if they were alive or dead; they were just drifting out, floating in an ocean of colors. Hundreds, maybe thousands. The thing gave a great sigh, and the screaming and rumbling stopped. Bodies continued to float out and settle gently on the streets of the city below. The colors thinned, and then were suddenly gone, like switching off a light. George could see everything now. Turning the pod around, he could see the Center. There were people running towards him. As he was being pulled back, he saw that they were medical personnel, running toward the people lying in the streets. Government people were running toward what was left of the thing, now rather small and deflated. Whatever the damned thing was, he'd apparently killed it. He felt strange, rather sorry for it. He almost *missed* it.

John felt no joy in the mission's success. He was angry at the world, heart pounding and mind throbbing. The only thought that gave him a bit of comfort was that there were more clouds yet. He still had a chance. There was still New York, and two more had formed in Chicago and Dallas.

As soon as he heard of the success, General Tchaikovsky hand-picked a group of scientists to follow the same procedure in other cities. At John's urging, he allowed George to take the one in New York. The "skin" of the Atlanta cloud was transported to Washington for study. Most of the victims there were dazed, but alive. They were sent to a government hospital for treatment. There were more scientists there than doctors.

George had had enough for a while. He was weak from the fight, and oddly depressed. All he really wanted was a few days of rest, some time to gather his thoughts. There was no doubt as to why John wanted him to take on the cloud in New York. And no doubt in his mind that it would be a much tougher operation.

"John, if I do this thing I'll need at least two days rest. I also need a pardon, to make sure that I'm not sent back to the Center when all of this is over."

"No problem at all. We're going to have to build something a little larger to penetrate this one, it will take some time. And if you survive, I'll have your pardon in my hand. *If* you survive."

"I know damn well what you're hoping for, but I will be back."

"But of course you will. I have all confidence in you."

Angie tried to argue George out of it during the flight back to Wilmington. By the time they reached her house, their relationship was strained. George went to bed and slept for twenty-four hours straight. Angie couldn't sleep at all. She watched the OWN news, and wasn't really surprised to see that the focus was on John rather than George. He was being touted as the hero, George merely a tool that John used in his brilliant scheme. Finally, she took a couple of pills and lay down beside him. She dreamt of the two men sword fighting in a dark cloud, with her watching, unable to move.

George felt more like himself after his extended rest. He apologized to Angie over coffee.

"I'm sorry that we argued, but you know that I have to do this. We can start all over again when it's over. Somewhere there's a place where we can be free. We're going to find that place, I promise.

"I'm putting my trust in you, George. I hope that you're right."

He reached across the table and kissed her. "I *am* right."

The sound of the cloud could be heard from the plane as they neared New York. They were forced to put on their suits in-air. It was a terrible sound, unlike anything they'd ever heard. Chanting, screaming, howling... a mixture of sounds that created a wall of hatred. John smiled a twisted smile. It sounded like home to him.

There were only three people in heavy suits when they reached the site. The cloud was a mile away, but as soon as the work had been finished all personnel had been moved even further back. Extended exposure to the sound, even through the soundproof suits, was maddening. George inspected the welds and bolts carefully. Satisfied, he asked John to take Angie back to the more distant site. John had one of the men take her back in a hovercraft. Sick to her stomach, she didn't argue. He himself wanted to stay. The swirling black-blue-purple, the sound... he couldn't bring himself to leave it. It was all he could do not to go closer. It was calling him. *"I love you, I need you... join with me..."*

Once he was sealed inside of the pod, the robotic arm began to unfurl in stages, slowly pushing him towards the cloud. The message he was getting was nothing like love. The closer he got, the louder the pounding in his brain became. Sorrow, loss, hurt, jealousy, pure hate... it seemed as if all evil was contained in this thing, and it was screaming to be let loose upon the world.

George began to sweat as he entered the dark mass. The radio was either silent or could not be heard above the noise. His vision blurred, he set the navigation to automatic, hoping that the settings he'd calculated were correct. After what seemed to be a very long time, the pale thing in the center became barely visible. It lay there throbbing, a giant maggot in the heart of the city. His head pounding, his breath shallow, he trained the laser on it. At the first cut, the shaking of the pod became too violent to continue. As well as the pod had been constructed, he knew that it wouldn't last much longer. Somehow he managed to re-set the laser onto 'blast', and fired. The explosion ripped the pod from the arm and sent him flying backwards. The screaming from the thing was deafening as he shot tumbling away from it. He blacked out.

John could hear its cries for help. "What have I done?" he thought. He began racing toward the cloud. Too late, he reached it just as it exploded, and was sent flying through the air. He landed face down on the pavement and didn't move.

George was in the Center, a ringing in his ears. Five bells, emergency. The panicked inmates were all trying to get out, but the exits were locked. A thick blue-black smoke came pouring out of the ventilation system. Suddenly, he opened his eyes. He was in the back of an ambulance, a medic on one side and Angie on the other. He slipped back into sleep.

The next time he awoke, he was in the ICU at the nearest hospital. Angie was sitting in a chair next to his bed.

"Hi, sleepyhead."

"Hi yourself. How did it go?"

"You're only banged up a little. They want to keep you here for a couple of days for observation."

"But how did the mission go? What happened? I don't remember anything after I set the laser on blast."

"The cloud is gone, that much was a success. You saved hundreds of lives. There were some casualties though. This was a lot different from the first cloud. George… the laser blast killed around one hundred people. But there was nothing else you could do, you know that."

"Damn."

"John is two rooms down. He's in much worse shape than you. For some reason he went running toward the thing just as it exploded. He's going to need plastic surgery as well as being treated for broken bones."

"What the hell could have possessed him to do something like that? I never gave him much credit for intelligence, but how could he do something *that* stupid? There's a lot more going on with these clouds than we know about yet. I need to be able to study them."

Angie got up, bent over, and kissed his forehead.

"Just rest right now. The other clouds are being taken care of. There'll be plenty of time to study them."

"Only if John keeps his word about that pardon. Is he conscious?"

"Not yet. But there are no guards waiting outside your door. I think we're okay for now."

John lay in his bed heavily medicated. His entire head was bandaged, leaving openings only at his nose and mouth. Oxygen tubes ran into his nostrils. He had fractured his skull, broken his left arm and leg, and cracked several ribs. Deep in his subconscious, a swirling mass of blue-black-violet sang to him. It was healing...

George left the hospital on a Tuesday. With John still unconscious, he was out of the loop. What was going on with the investigations? What were the scientists learning? And what of the people who had been rescued? Angie came in and led him to the bedroom. Smiling, she kissed him and whispered "Just don't overdo it."

Afterward, they sat at the table talking.

"I need to get back to work, George. The doctor will call as soon as John regains consciousness. Stay close, okay? I don't want anything to happen to you.'"

"I will. When all of this is over... I love you, Angie."

"I love you too, George, with all my heart."

Alone, he turned on the news. Surprisingly, there was actual *news* for a change.

"Although far from complete, preliminary studies show that the cloud-producing husks were somehow formed by strong checked emotions. Evidently, we have met the enemy and he is us. The government is already forming committees to look into possible solutions. It is not impossible that Law12 concerning the expression of love and hate may be on its way out."

In the hospital, John's eyes popped open. He didn't just feel better, he felt magnified. He felt like a lion. The first thing he did was to place a call to see if any of the Centers were still in operation. They weren't. The clouds had been destroyed, but the Centers' operations had been put on hold. He pulled out the oxygen lines and IV tubes and walked down the hall, looking like a monster from an old horror movie. When an orderly tried to help him, he shoved him aside and kept walking purposefully to the nearest exit.

Dr. Jarvis called and spoke to George. He was as shaken as any doctor he'd ever heard. He told him that John had left the hospital against medical advice. Even though his bones were healing at a phenomenal rate, the last scan had shown that there was still swelling in the brain. There was no family to call. George suggested calling the WHO and letting them know what was going on. They wouldn't let him come back to work until he was properly released.

George put the phone down and stared at it. Somehow he knew that John wasn't going back to work. He sat down and waited. The sweet singing began, so far down in his subconscious that he at first didn't notice it. Slowly, the world looked brighter, more colorful. He felt at peace, but strong and powerful at the same time. George felt that he could conquer the world with love and peace. It was a strange, exhilarating feeling.

He called Angie at work and told her to go to her sister's house, or better yet, a motel. She reluctantly agreed.

At home, John stood in front of the bathroom mirror, cutting off his bandages. He smiled when he saw what was beneath them; a broken nose, mottled swollen skin, one eye drooping. His head had been shaved in the hospital as well, making him look even more monstrous. "I like it," he thought, and smiled again. The color of his eyes had changed to black. "Georgie… Georgie, I'm coming for you…" he cooed in a sickly-sweet voice, and laughed out loud.

Darkness fell as George sat and stared out of the front door. Soon after, he heard a crackling sound, followed by thin streaks of pale blue light. John stood outside, his hands raised toward the sky. Flashes of lightning reached from the sky to his fingertips. Rain and thunder followed. George didn't recognize the voice as John's when he called to him.

"C'mon out and play, Georgie…"

He gathered his strength and stepped outside. As he approached John, he was suddenly knocked to the ground by a powerful punch to the jaw. Then John was on top of him, throwing quick sharp jabs at his face and ribs. George managed to kick him off and land a couple of punches himself.

As the men fought, two clouds formed around them, darkness and light. They seemed lost in the clouds, the clouds themselves pushing and shoving against each other. Each was trying to envelope the other. Sensors in the air attracted to the powerful emotions were sent spinning. The multi-colored cloud around George seemed to be weakening, overpowered by the huge dark one. He felt himself being sucked into the dark cloud, even as he continued to fight. It was sick and black, and sapped his strength. He tried hard to think of Angie, of love, of a bright future, but the cloud was like a disease. It howled like madness, overwhelming his senses. He was weakening.

Suddenly, headlights appeared. Angie stepped out of the car. She held her breath at the scene before her. It was much like the dream she'd had, the two men fighting while she watched. At last finding her voice, she called out to George. Hearing her through the chaos, he felt a new burst of energy, his strength renewed. He couldn't afford to lose. "Losing is not an option," he thought. Falling on top of John, he put his hands around his throat and tightened them. The dark cloud began to diminish, the light one to grow stronger. As the life left John's body, the dark cloud swirled down and into his head. Suddenly, it was gone. The rainbow cloud expanded, larger and larger, until it burst into the night sky like fireworks. At that moment, everyone in the world received a tiny bit of it. Not much, but enough for many couples to suddenly turn to each other and say "I love you."

"You knew I'd come, didn't you?"

"What took you so long?"

The dawn was the most beautiful anyone had ever seen. A new feeling of love, peace and trust permeated the world. The government quickly decided to discontinue the emotional rehabilitation program, and declared that love was now acceptable; even the most passionate kind. However, they did declare that those convicted of actually carrying out hate related activity would be sent to the criminal prison units on the moon. Even politicians.

The studies on the cloud survivors were dropped, and they were allowed to go home. Although the scientists, including George, studied the remains, it was never determined how the clouds had actually formed. George had an idea, but it wasn't scientific. He never presented it to his colleagues.

A generation passed, and it all seemed like a distant dream to those who'd lived through it. But they never stopped telling the story, hoping that some future generation wouldn't repeat the mistakes of the past.

This was all long before the dark cloud on the moon began to form...

Blackout Days

1

I remember the Blackout Days, when I was young and machines thrummed. Dark days, yes, but there was the tiniest streak of light on the horizon called hope. Baseball players wore black uniforms; it was easier to see them against the floodlights. We didn't have pets; anything was considered fair game for the table in those lean times. But we kept the machines running, and focused on that strip of light on the horizon.

Looking back now after so many years, it's amazing that we took it all in stride. But it was just the way things were. I was twelve when I began work in the factory, my schooling done. But I was proud; I was doing something important. I was feeding the machines, making sure they never stopped. I didn't really know at the time what might happen if they stopped, but I knew it was something bad. It was every citizen's duty to contribute, to keep those machines working. I was glad to do it, even though my hearing is diminished now from the noise.

Every night when I walked home, I'd check the horizon to see if that strip of light had grown wider. I wasn't disappointed when it hadn't, though, I didn't really expect it. They said it might be years before we saw daylight again. When I slept, I dreamed of bright blue skies and green grass. The younger kids had never seen what it was like in the before times, so they had nothing to miss. I thought maybe they were lucky.

One night I ventured out into the Zone, and almost got myself killed. It was only then that I realized the scope of the fighting, and how close it was to us. That scared me. Before, I hadn't let things bother me much, but now I listened when the president came on and talked. I started listening when the adults talked about survival and "worst possible outcomes." My childhood was gone, just like that. I worked harder, studied the horizon more closely, and kept my mouth shut and my eyes and ears open. Sometimes things become too real. Some things, once lost, can never be regained.

I met Mingus in '093, when I was fourteen. A new face was always big news, since all but absolutely necessary travel had been prohibited for years. I found a seat beside him at dinner and introduced myself. Once we got past the pleasantries, he told me that he'd been living with an aunt in a small borderline town called Bierville. When she died, he'd moved here to live with his only other living relative, a cousin. When I heard the name Plastikow, I knew immediately who his cousin was; a small grim man who already had the allotted two children. I guess this was a special circumstance. Still, I couldn't see him being happy about the situation. Harmon Plastikow was not one to be happy about much of anything.

"How do you like it here so far?"

"It's a little different, but I'll get used to it."

"Different how?"

"I don't know, it just seems more… intense."

"I couldn't say. I've never left Wormwood. First there was no reason to, then the Blackout happened… I've often wondered what other places are like, though."

"Some were beautiful, man. I say were because all this time without sunlight had to have destroyed their beauty."

"Yeah, I remember the flowers and colors, the autumn leaves… it was all here until six years ago."

"You think they'll ever come back?

"Well, nothing lasts forever. Some things just seem to."

The whistle blew, and we had to empty the remains from our trays and get back to work. Neither of us was sure what kind of meat we'd just eaten, and neither of us was very interested in finding out. Some things are better left unknown.

A siren interrupted the second half of our shift. We all fell into place and marched down to the shelter. We knew the drill. It had happened many times before, never anything to worry about. The false alarm or drill or whatever it was put us behind schedule, and we worked hard to catch up. The hours flew by, but we managed. The machines had to be fed.

I awoke on my day off feeling something I rarely allowed myself to feel; dissatisfaction, anger, sorrow. All the negative emotions seemed to collide with each other, making a huge ball of angst in my soul. I'd been dreaming about the before times, when there was light and color everywhere. As I waited for the coffee to brew, I tried to give myself a pep talk. "Nothing lasts forever, even these dark days." It wasn't working. I knew that so many things that had to be deferred until better times would be lost forever. It was selfish, I knew, but I was tired of waiting. I wanted something I hadn't had since the Blackout Days began… happiness. I chuckled bitterly about how this world of constant night was still divided into night and day. It was eight in the morning now, but it looked the same as it would at eight this evening.

After an hour of allowing myself to grieve, I put it aside and went on with the day. Life was still being lived. There was a concert in the park today, with people and food and drink. "Just what I need," I thought. I remembered something I'd seen in the museum, when paper was made from trees and printed on. Charlie Brown and the Little Red-Haired Girl. Maybe *my* little red-haired girl would be in the park today. I knew that my mom wouldn't be going. She was a zombie since Dad had left to fight, going through the routine of her days emotionless. She only went out for groceries, and disliked even that small task. She wouldn't take the pills that the doctor had prescribed, either. She thought that it would be wrong to make herself artificially happy with Dad having to face every day in danger. I missed him, too, but he'd been gone for so long now that his memory was beginning to fade. I remembered more of his essence than the man himself; a warm glowing ball of colors that made me happy.

I stopped thinking of him and got dressed. I couldn't allow myself to get into another funk. Mingus was off work today, and we planned to meet at the park early so we could get a good spot. The band was going to be Every Death's A Suicide. When I stepped outside, I could swear that the grey horizon line was just a little wider.

4

The band was amazing. They appeared out of a rolling fog, all in black with faces painted white. A simulated thunderstorm raged around them as they played. At the most exciting moments, a black light flashed. The music was a strange serenade in minor chords, a sound that can best be described as Goth-Metal. There was really no label to apply to it, though; they had invented a new sound.

Mingus loved it even more than I did. When it was over, he kept crying out for more. After two encores, I knew there would be no more, but he shouted until I began to worry about him. At last he stopped as the crowd thinned. He looked at me and spoke: "They're gods."

The rest of our time in the park was a surreal experience. Something had happened, I wasn't sure what. Maybe it just hit me how insane it was to be eating hot dogs in the dark, with crowds of people you could barely see. The floodlights should have come on after the band, but for some reason they never did. I thought that I might have seen her, out in the crowds, but it was hard to tell. I couldn't get close enough to her to speak, anyway.

I went to bed that night feeling as happy as I'd ever allowed myself to be, and dreamed in bright colors.

Monday was a big let-down; back to feeding the machines, their song so loud that I couldn't even listen to music in my mind. Words like "endless" and "pointless" kept coming to me instead. Mingus wasn't there. I couldn't help but be a little concerned after his behavior yesterday. The day dragged on to its conclusion, and I went home feeling empty.

"Somewhere out there, there are color hoarders." I felt it in my bones. I wondered what the truth about everything was. Everyone knew not to trust what the government told you, or what the news was allowed to report. These would be dark days even if the world was exploding in color… it just wouldn't be as noticeable.

Suddenly the sirens broke my reverie. Not just the usual one, they seemed to be coming from everywhere. There was an urgency in getting down into the shelter. Something was happening. I thought of my mom, and Mingus, but there was nothing that I could do but hope they were okay.

The war had come to us. The buffer zone that had seemed so secure yesterday had been breached. The uneasy faces on the monitors in the shelter belied their soothing commentary. I felt that we were on a sinking ship, with the captain standing in the center crying "All is well!" Not even the most naïve believed the bullshit we were being told. A murmur went through the crowd when men in black uniforms were seen briefly on the monitors, then only static. We were being overrun, it seemed.

The machines upstairs were stopped and growing cold. Silence. People seemed afraid even to speak. I thought of how relatively careless we'd been only yesterday, and wished that I'd allowed myself to be happier while I had the chance. I feared that "happy" wouldn't be in our vocabulary for a while.

I thought about her, the girl whose name I didn't even know. Where was she? Was she okay? I hoped so. I felt so powerless… what could a fourteen year old boy do in this situation? "He can become a man," I thought. I knew that I needed to step up, somehow, but I really didn't know how to go about it. I needed to think, to clear my mind of everything but solving the problem at hand.

I walked into the farthest corner of the room, away from everyone as much as possible. Sitting down, I put my head in my hands and began to think. Finally, I had a coherent thought; what our troops needed was something fantastic to rally them. Something like a blast of natural light and color to pull them up from the darkness. But the time was now, and I had no idea how to go about it. What could be done?

It hit me suddenly. Powerful music and a kick-ass light show might make a difference. At least it could change their attitudes, give them a reason to go on. I had to find Mingus. He'd know how to set it up. As I began walking through the crowds looking for him, I made plans as to where and how we could accomplish this concert for the damned.

I spotted Mingus' head above all the others in the crowd. He was possibly the tallest person in the city. Once we'd waded through and got close enough to talk, I told him my idea. He snickered a little bit, telling me that was the dumbest shit he'd ever heard. I finally convinced him by asking if anyone else had a plan at all, good or bad. "Okay," he said, "this really shouldn't be that hard to set up. Useless, but something to do besides sit on our asses and wait." He took the lead from there, finding the band and the necessary technicians. I helped with the location; it had to be right out in the danger zone to make an impact. We had to pull this thing together quickly, or it would be too late to have a chance at working. The band said that it was a suicide mission, laughing like hell. "We're the perfect band for it."

There was a lot more to set up than I'd realized, and it was being done in a war zone. All was quiet for now, though, and everyone worked quickly. Roadies, technicians… the band had called upon everyone they knew. I was still in awe of them, and couldn't believe this was really happening. The main thing I wanted to concentrate on besides the music was light. We needed light from every source possible. Enough light to make people remember what it was like before the great blackout. A reminder that working together, we could accomplish great things, and much sooner.

There were military vehicles pulling into the area just as preparations were finished. Without any hype, the band began to play. "Every death's a suicide/ Every word's a lie" The music thundered, and the light show was later compared to those that our great-great grandfathers had seen in the twentieth century. A crowd quickly gathered; civilians, soldiers from both sides too enraptured to fight. It was an impromptu truce. By the end of the long show, the sky shone brightly all over the area, about two miles of real-looking daylight. Our soldiers could have used this as a chance to re-group and drive the intruders back out, but everyone seemed to have forgotten about war. The band had been playing for two hours straight, afraid that all this goodwill would stop with the music. At last, they announced that they were going to take a break. The last thing they said before leaving the stage was "Everyone hug the person next to you!"

Strangely enough, it worked. It was the beginning of a peace movement that would sweep across both sides, forcing the leaders to the negotiating table. It was the beginning of the end of the Blackout days; light and color were eventually restored all over the world. Mingus and myself, along with Every Death's a Suicide, were given medals. "Finally," I thought, "a story with a happy ending." By the way, the girl's name was Hope, and she's been my wife now for twenty years.

The Tell

1

Ponchoboy and Rangergirl each had a big slice of heaven pie at the Shangri-La Diner. Afterwards, they rode out of town on a mule, backwards. No one knew why. It was the next day that the sky was colorless. It amazed most people. The blue was gone! Oysterboy and Starfishgirl stood outside the pink hotel looking up in wonder. Where did the sky go? It's still there, it just kind of... not. A generic little girl stood nearby, crying.

"God forgot to color in the sky!" she bawled.

"There, there" A lady in a big straw hat patted the little girl's head. "I'll call him and tell him about his mistake."

Oysterboy and Starfishgirl stepped over the pink-painted stones that bordered the pink hotel, past a few scraggly palmettos, and stumbled down the slope to the dazzle of the white sand beach. The ocean was amazing. You could see far, and far, and far. Little creatures swam and crawled everywhere. Oysterboy and Starfishgirl felt like they were on an alien planet, seeing things for the first time. They looked at the sea, at each other, back at the sea.

"I think I'll speak French today," Oysterboy announced.

"I think I would like that," Starfishgirl replied.

"Gengirl, I'm sorry" said the straw hat lady. "911 says it isn't an emergency, and God's number is unlisted."

Across the borderline in the badlands, Ponchoboy and Rangergirl huddled in a boxcar, drinking wine with Eclipseboy. The sky began to turn black. Maw-Maw told them to watch out for the holes in the bottom of the car. The train sped on, the blackness spread.

"This isn't fun anymore" mumbled Ponchoboy, and stopped scribbling notes for his epic novel. He crumbled each page and threw them down the holes.

Far away, Oysterboy heard the train's lonesome whistle in his sleep. His dreams turned from pink hotels and colorless skies to friends and family, jumping off the train one by one.

...

Oysterboy got up and looked out the window. The sky was black, but the twinkling stars were all in their places. He felt a heavy weight, the weight of a thousand voices in his head. "I'm cold." "I'm lonely." "I'm sick." "I'm poor." "I don't feel loved." Across the sky these voices cried, drifting into Oysterboy's head. Suddenly his room at the pink hotel seemed shabbier.

Four in the morning. A wave of homesickness slipped over the voices in his head and settled in his heart. He walked outside so that he could hear the comforting sound of the ocean. His childhood home was miles away, long abandoned. The pink hotel and Starfishgirl were his world now. "Why do I hear these voices?" he thought, "Why do they bother me?" Then he thought of all his dear friends, and how much he missed them. His voice mingled with the others. "I have holes in my heart."

The voices became gull's cries as dawn broke over the horizon. Starfishgirl stood silently beside him. He took her hand, and they watched the sun rise. The weight didn't lift. The sky was colorless again today, but everyone seemed to be used to it already. "I love you, Oysterboy." "I love you too, Starfishgirl." They sat on a rock and watched the sun make its way across the sky in silence.

2

One-eyed Willie sat resting his bony ass on the sack of ashes he'd been carrying. The road to Pink was long, and for the most part untraveled. The stars had told him to go, though, and who was he to argue with them? A growing speck of dust down the road caught his attention. "I hope it's a truck!" he thought, "or even a mule cart." It was indeed a mule cart, driven by Pawpaw and Scoutgirl. Willie gratefully climbed into the back, rested his over-sized head on the bag, and fell straight to sleep. He awoke an hour later feeling much more rested, and made small talk with Pawpaw and Scoutgirl about the strange weather. Then he was in Pink, saying goodbye and beginning the short walk to the Rox River.

Willie sat down by the riverbank, waiting for the stars to make the right alignment. Around 3:00 AM, the stars locked in place and shimmered down upon him. He poured the contents of his bag into the river, in three equal increments. Each time the ashes sank, a white dove flew up and off into the sky. Willie was relieved and overjoyed; he knew that for once, he'd done something right. By 4:00 AM, the wind was blowing the stars about until they formed a funnel. Willie reached up and was happily taken away. He hoped the sky would be blue, there. Silence reigned until morning.

...

Oysterboy was restless again, wrestling with fevered dreams and painful headaches. He saw the beast first in one of those dreams. It was grey, the size of a huge possum. Its beady black eyes reflected some great need, some deep longing. Its long muzzle was filled with sharp, evenly-pointed teeth. It nuzzled against Oysterboy in bed, grazing teeth across his arm. It left sometimes to sniff out others, but always came crawling back to nuzzle Oysterboy. Starfishgirl woke up, and looked sadly at his fitful sleep. She felt helpless, but ashamed as well for her thoughts; "You never speak French to me anymore." It was true, though. The fact was that Oysterboy barely spoke at all anymore. Starfishgirl got out of bed and read the last poem he'd written for her, before the sky changed.

"Tin cup rattle, see how the stars align tonight?
Wooden table thunk, look, they're smiling!
Scrape of chair on wooden floor, one just winked at me
Meager meal by candlelight, but so happy, so happy
These are the days of wonder and love, the little days
The bright spots sandwiched in between work and boredom
Between births and deaths and catastrophes, these are the days
that sing
Leave the dishes for the kitchen elves, come to bed, she says
And the stars really do wink and smile"

Climbing back into bed, she lay there awake, stoking his hair, waiting for morning. She knew that some beast shared their bed, but she couldn't see it. It didn't keep her from hating it. Oysterboy finally calmed down. He was dreaming of three white doves pecking at the grey beast.

Oysterboy and Starfishgirl walked down the planked sidewalks, looking at all the things they'd seen so often. The crooked, wildly painted houses, the strange little shops, the carnival rides and food stands beachside. Balloons were still tethered everywhere from the last Finding's Day. Neither one said it, but both were thinking it; how much prettier and happier everything had looked beneath blue skies. Oysterboy caught a glimpse of a grey beast snuffling around a doorstep, but when he turned his head it was gone. "Things fall apart," he thought. He noticed details; peeling paint, warped wood, ragged clowns and gypsies looking at their feet instead of making eye contact. They placed a large order in the Spirits Shoppe. Tonight would be a busy night at the Pink Bar, but they had the feeling that it wouldn't be a good night.

They opened the doors early, impatient to get the night over and done with. They missed Ponchoboy, Rangergirl and Eclipseboy. They would have come early and talked to them over free beer until the crowd arrived. As it was, no one came until the sun was almost down. The usual crowd straggled in; Gypsies, clowns, carneys, townsfolk. Seven Hooded Ones took a table in the corner and drank silently. Music played, but no one danced. They all seemed intent on one thing- getting as drunk as possible as quickly as possible. These were not good days in Pink.

Oysterboy dreamed again of the grey beast. It was trying to push its clawed feet into his skin and wrap them around his bones. The three white doves aggravated it enough to keep it from accomplishing its mission, but they weren't strong enough to pull it up and carry it away. The stars were pinholes in the black cloth of the sky. Oysterboy awoke early, exhausted and with his head pounding. When he splashed water onto his face, he noticed how flat and lifeless his eyes looked. Starfishgirl had left a note, saying that she'd gone digging for clams. She sat on a rock and cried instead.

"Comment allez-vous?" he asked.
"Don't." she replied. "It is not a good day for French."
"I know. It is not a good day for anything."
"Maybe we should go see The Bald One."
"No. He sells only dreams. I've had enough of those."
"Who, then? We need someone. There has to be someone with wisdom to help us."

"We need to see Maw-Maw."

"But she lives in the sky now!"

"We have to see her. She's the only one who can make things right again."

"All right. We'll gather the stones today, and cast the tell tonight."

...

The stones were laid out on the beach in the prescribed fashion, the fire burning in the center. Oysterboy and Starfishgirl danced around the perimeter, throwing incense and whispering the secret chant. They began slowly, gradually picking up speed. They could not stop once it was begun, no matter how long it might take. Their eyes sparkled, and the stars responded. They seemed to dance with them, faster and faster. When Oysterboy and Starfishgirl were at the point of exhaustion, a great billow of white smoke erupted from the flame. Maw-Maw's gentle eyes and smiling countenance looked down at them.

"Hello, my children. I've been waiting to hear from you."

"You know the problem, then. How do I rid myself of the beast, and bring the color back to the sky?"

"This is not a small problem that you have. It will take a lot of work and strength to make things right again. However, the stars have chosen you to do it. Can you?"

"We have to."

"You two must work together. It will not be easy. Your dreams tonight will tell you what you must do. I have to go now. I love you, my children."

Oysterboy and Starfishgirl embraced, very tired but on fire with new hope. The stars were fading into a new day as they walked back up to the pink hotel.

The aura of sadness and decay had set in into all of Pink. From the industrialized north, the farmlands to the south and the jagged mountains of the west it could be felt. Things seemed to be winding down, pressing in. More people were seeing the little grey beasts, but no one was talking about it.

Oysterboy and Starfishgirl closed down the bar early that night, and made themselves a small sleeping potion. They lay on the bed hand-in-hand, waiting for sleep with its promised dreams. Soon, they were walking down a long dark road. The tall trees on each side arched together over the top, shutting out moon and stars. They walked towards a distant blue light. It was far away, but their dream-legs took them there quickly.

Skullcapboy and Goatsheadboy were oblivious to the dream-people peering in the window of their house. Oysterboy and Starfishgirl looked in amazement at the decayed palace. There were dusty old tomes everywhere, potion bottles, old maps. Strangest of all was a round table in the corner, where six skeletons wearing party hats sat around a moldy black birthday cake, its candles sunken at odd angles. Cobwebs covered everything, even the two living tenants of the house. They stopped for a moment from poring over some decayed old book to sniff the air like dogs. Oysterboy and Starfishgirl held their breath, and the moment passed.

An eerie blue light played over everything, and finally the two found its source. A huge iron bell sat in another corner, blue light shining sickly from around its bottom edge. They had found the blue of the sky. Just as a beady-eyed creature turned its head towards them, they awoke. Wordlessly, they looked at each other, knowing what had to be done.

Skullcapboy and Goatsheadboy had been chased to the edge of the mountains long ago for practicing bad magic. The gentle people of Pink couldn't bear to send them all the way to the Outlands, and so there they had stayed, scheming their revenge. Now they had the sky, and were releasing the beasts. They had to be stopped soon, or all of Pink would fall apart.

There were a few rusted motorized vehicles left from the Before, and Moonboy had one. It was a truck large enough to carry all the people to do the Circle. He agreed, and they managed to find enough friends to make the twelve needed. They made their plans as they rode down the long dark road. It didn't take long, and they spent the rest of the time singing the songs of The Old Ones. The songs that they'd heard over and over began to take on new meaning, enlightening under the new circumstances. "Ticking away the moments that make up a dull day..." They rode on. The arched branches of the trees were like lovers holding hands in the darkness.

"Starfishgirl, never forget; death may conquer life, but it can never conquer love."

She nodded. She knew.

Loudmouth

1

Mawgish and Snuffy-Muffy sat on the front porch, spitting snuff juice into empty Peach Snuff cans. Ronnie-Bob ambled around the corner, grinning a grin. He held his little brother Boo-Boo's hand. Mawgish could see that Boo-Boos diaper was still weighed down.
"I told you to go home and tell your mama to change Boo-Boo's diaper!"
Ronnie-Bob slunk back around the corner and waited a few seconds, then came walking back into the yard.
Snuffy-Muffy's face was red with anger.
"Take Boo-Boo home and tell your mama to change his diaper!"
Ronnie-Bob finally gave in and went home, dragging Boo-Boo behind. He'd been having fun at the old folk's house and didn't want to leave. Even at four years old, he knew that the magic would be broken by the time he could return. They'd been telling stories and singing songs. By the time he got back, they'd probably be inside fixing supper or something. He knew his mama probably wouldn't let him go back anyway. He was right.

2

Ronnie-Bob was playing around with something in the living room, maybe a bug. When his mama got off the phone, he knew something was wrong.
"Your Paw-Paw's dead."
She started crying. Ronnie-Bob had never seen his mama cry before. He wasn't sure how to react. He laughed a little, just from not knowing what else to do. He didn't really know what "dead" meant. Not until he saw Paw-Paw in his coffin with flowers all around, and grown-ups crying. He knew then that it meant he'd never see his Paw-Paw again. He cried a little bit then.

3

That night was the first time he heard Loudmouth's voice. He heard it through the darkness as he lay in bed trying to go to sleep. It was an eerie sound; it spooked the hell out of him. It was far away, like a train whistle, but it was coming closer. He wondered if everybody else heard it, or if it was all in his head. Nobody said anything, so he decided it must be in his head. He heard it every night from then on. He thought maybe it had something to do with Paw-Paw's death. They had moved away to a new house, and he couldn't visit Mawgish and Snuffy-Muffy anymore. Things were changing. He decided that he didn't like change. He didn't like Loudmouth either, but there was nothing a six-year-old could do about it. He wanted to run away and be a pirate, but he wasn't sure how to go about it. There wasn't an ocean nearby.

4

Ronnie-Bob lay on the living room floor, drawing pictures of what he thought Loudmouth might look like. He looked like a guy wearing a ghost sheet, with a big yawning mouth… and for some reason, a green army cap on his head. His mama always bragged on his pictures. That made him want to do even better. He told her about Loudmouth, but she didn't seem to understand. Probably no grown-up would. He knew somehow that it was one of those things only children could know about. Boo-Boo knew about it. They would be getting a new brother or sister soon, and he bet they'd know about it too. At least once they stopped being a baby and became a real person. Boo-Boo was four now, and he could talk to him.

The new baby was a girl named Shern. Ronnie-Bob and Boo-Boo felt old and wise, and were very protective of their new sister. Ronnie-Bob missed Mawgish and Snuffy-Muffy's songs and stories about the olden days. Mama read him Greek mythology, about things like people being served their baby cooked up and eating it without knowing. He didn't tell her, but it creeped him out. He'd rather have heard Mawgish's stories about when her mother was a little girl during the civil war. About horse-and-buggy days, things like that.

6

The night of the day Willy was killed on his bicycle, Loudmouth was really close. Willy was the preacher's son, and Ronnie-Bob knew him from school. He was a good kid. He didn't have to go to the funeral, and he was glad. He'd already seen Paw-Paw and Uncle Finger in their coffins, and he didn't want to see any more. People didn't look like themselves when they were dead. They looked like department store mannequins made up to look like the person they used to be. He pulled the covers over his head and waited for Loudmouth to shut up. His mama came in to kiss him goodnight.
"Are you alright, Ronnie-Bob?"
"Yeah, I'm alright." he lied.
Ronnie-Bob was nine now, and beginning to realize that he'd never been all right. Maybe he never would be.

Killer

Prologue

June 23rd, 1953

 Ronnie was walking aimlessly up and down the rows of corn the day
his grandmother died. Suddenly a murder of crows flew up and startled
him. Turning to run back toward the house, he found himself staring at
the scarecrow. In a black hat and long black duster it looked like a
monster that had an affinity for eating children. He ran as quickly as he
was able back to the house, imagining the monster right behind him. He
hurried in, slamming the door behind him. His mother was sitting on
the sofa, teary eyed. She said simply "Your grandma's dead." He felt
the crows flying into his head as he stood there, speechless. That was
the day his sorrow took form, and it was in the form of crows.

Chapter One: Crows

July 22nd, 1954: Alison, NC

The light was blinding bright, blowing away the night like a bomb. The night that now seemed so surreal and strange. Ronnie had dreamed again of burning down the house, seen his parents succumb to the smoke without even waking up. The smoldering ruins looked perfectly natural now, the blackened metal stove and water heater cartoonish. He thought about the movie theatre cartoons. He'd miss them. It was almost all that he'd miss. He wouldn't miss the noisy house with all the yelling and fighting. That was what had finally done it, the explosions in his head from the clanging, banging noise. Ronnie wished that he'd saved his little green army men. They were in a blackened lump on the stone porch. He'd really meant to take them. He'd been so entranced by the flames that he'd forgotten about everything else.

It was time to leave now, to walk through the pumpkin field to the woods on the other side. Ronnie remembered how the scarecrow had scared him when he was younger, and there were rows of corn instead of pumpkins. He was headed for the train tracks. He knew about hopping trains. His older brother Jay had told him all about it before he finally left for good. There was an old carnival up in Helix where Jay had worked once. He figured he'd try to find it and get a job there. Walking among the pumpkins, he almost felt normal. Birds chattered overhead in the bright July sun. He thought that some of them were trying to talk to him, but he didn't know the language.

The woods darkened the sky, and the birds here sounded darker as well. He passed old tombstones leaning at crazy angles. Beloved wife, beloved son, all of them were from the 1800s to the early 1900s. The biggest ones were all Morrison. They'd been a rich family who owned factories long ago. Some of his aunts and uncles had worked for them. He remembered stories. He didn't think anyone was sad that the Morrisons were all dead now. The thought suddenly hit him that his parents were really dead. There was no turning back, even if he wanted to. Suddenly tired, he decided to lie down on the soft leaf-covered ground and take a nap.

He dreamed that stars were talking to him, twinkling around his head. They were warm and loving, and wanted to take care of him. That dream faded, and he awoke with a start. The last dream had been of his father beating him with a belt while his mother looked on, hands covering her mouth. He realized that he'd slept the day away and had lost his bearings. An owl spoke to him through the darkness. He answered, trying to imitate the owl's sound. His throat was dry, though, and his stomach empty. Fully awake now, he realized that he was almost out of the woods. Not only that, but he could see a dim light in the distance. A house, maybe, where he could find some food and drink. He walked towards the light, a little faster now. The owl seemed to be following him, although he couldn't see it in the darkness. That was OK with Ronnie, he could use a friend.

Out of the woods, he walked through a little garden behind an unpainted old farmhouse. There were big juicy tomatoes growing there, and he picked one and stuffed it into his mouth. It was the best tomato he'd ever had. He walked quietly up to the window where the light was shining and looked in. An old woman was dozing in a rocking chair, a black cat on her lap. Suddenly the cat leapt off her lap, startling both of them. The old woman saw his face at the window, and picked up a shotgun that he hadn't noticed standing against the wall beside her.
"Damned thieves and scoundrels! Get out of here before I fill you full of buckshot!"

Ronnie ducked down and ran, crouching, to the nearest tree.

She couldn't see him when she walked out on the porch holding the gun.
"That's right" she muttered, "better git from here."

His hopes of a sweet old lady serving him apple pie and ice cream were dashed. But he knew she had food and water in there, and he knew that he needed it. He sat behind the tree and waited a long time. At last the light in the house went out

.

Ronnie had The Dream again. A hundred little children standing in a vast field all dressed in white, each holding a black balloon. They released them all at once, and they floated up into the sky. Time seemed to slow down as he watched them rise, but he knew what was coming. The balloons suddenly turned into cawing crows, thousands of them darkening the sky.

When he opened his eyes he was in the house. The old lady lay motionless in her bed, a pillow over her face. The cat sat guard beside her. He went into the kitchen and ate some beans and fried chicken cold from her refrigerator. Then he grabbed a few cans from the cabinet and wrapped them in a towel, remembering to find the can-opener. He wished that he could carry more, but this would have to do. He finished a bottle of milk, rinsed it out, and filled it with water. Finding some money in her purse, he jammed it into his pockets. The house was so quiet and peaceful now that he hated to leave. He felt sorry for the cat, and put some food and water out for it. He didn't feel sorry for the old woman. All she had to do was be nice, but she wasn't. He walked out and didn't look back. He was afraid that he might see crows following him.

The sun rose shortly after Ronnie began walking the ten miles to Monroe where the train yard was. The road was little-used, but he hid in the bushes whenever he heard a car, just in case. He was sure that they assumed that he had died in the fire, but better to be safe. He rationed the water, even though the day was hot and muggy. Stopping when he got hungry, he opened a can of Vienna sausages and ate them with his fingers. His thoughts wandered as he walked. He thought about his army men. He knew that at twelve he was too old to be playing with them, but they symbolized something that he just couldn't let go of. The fighting was in Korea last, but he fought and re-fought World War II. Americans against Nazis, good versus evil. In this world, the good guys always won. There was something satisfying to him about that. He thought of his Grandma. Before she died last year, her house was a sanctuary of peace and quiet that he could escape to now and then. He remembered her odd old sayings, like "Don't wash clothes on New Year's Day, you'll be washing for a funeral," or "When it rains while the sun is shining, the devil's beating his wife." She was good to him, though. She cooked the best chicken and dumplings he'd ever had. Thinking about it made him hungry again, but a can of beans wasn't going to do the trick. Walking, walking, thinking, thinking. Ronnie figured that by nightfall he was close to Monroe, so he went a short distance into some woods, ate the beans, and fell asleep.

It was not a restful night. The stars twinkled around his head like fireflies as he fell asleep, soothing him, but they didn't stay long. He was fighting someone in his dreams, someone he couldn't quite see.

Once he awoke, thinking that he was in his old bed at home. Falling back to sleep, he dreamed of witches with black cats, and crows over a pumpkin field. He dreamed of a scarecrow chasing him through the darkness. He dreamed of school, with everyone pointing and laughing at him. At last, just before dawn, he dreamed of being in his grandmother's feather bed, sinking down deep into sleep. Ronnie didn't want to wake from that dream, but he did, just as the sun crept over the horizon.

Ronnie ate a breakfast of beans, washing them down with the last of the water. He tried to remember everything that Jay had told him about hopping trains. He remembered that the crew at the Monroe train yard were nice guys, and was sure they'd help him catch the right train.

He passed a pond just before the Monroe town limits, drank, and re-filled his water bottle. He wasn't sure how he'd find the train yard without asking someone, and he really didn't want to go into the town proper. Still, he did have money, and he'd love to have a decent meal. Ronnie had never been to a restaurant alone before. Maybe he could find a little diner somewhere, eat, and get the information he needed. He walked into the small town trying to look as inconspicuous as a twelve year old runaway could.

Chapter Two: Trains

A dirty-faced boy in an olive green tee shirt and jeans walked into the diner. The bell rung over the door as he entered, catching the waitress's attention. She was a middle-aged woman with too much rouge on her cheeks.

"Hey, Big Boy, what can I do for you?" she smiled.

Ronnie sat down at the counter. He was happy that the place was empty except for the two of them. "A burger, some fries and a coke, please."

"You got money?" she asked, her eyebrows arching a bit.

Ronnie showed her the bills in his pocket.

"Well, you got yourself some lunch, then." The smile returned. "Hey, Sam, need a burger and fries out here" she spoke loudly to the back.

"Gotcha" came the reply.

"Never seen you around here before, Big Boy. You on vacation?"

"Yes ma'am, kinda. My Grandma and me are looking for my uncle. He works at the train yard."

"Where's your Grandma?"

"She's taking a nap in the car. She gave me this money to get something to eat, and ask where the train yard is."

"Un-huh. Well, you're not far from it. Just go north on Main and there's a street that crosses it at the second stoplight called Railroad Street. Take a left there and you can't miss it."

"Thank you, ma'am."

"Burgers up!" sounded out of the back. She went over to the pass and came back with his food. He ate voraciously and had two cokes.

"You're not shooting me a line of bull about being here with your Grandma, are you? I don't see no car waiting outside for you."

Ronnie looked her in the eyes, and she suddenly had a vision of her face being pushed into the deep-fat fryer. "Nevermind, none of my business anyway. That'll be one-twenty-five." She felt a great sense of relief when he left. "Sam, get out here! Did you see that boy?"

"How could I see him, I ain't been out here."

"There's something wrong with him. I hope I never have to look into eyes like that again, I tell ya."

He watched from the window to see if she went for the phone. She put her elbows on the counter and stayed there. Good. He'd heard the crows calling in the distance there for a few minutes. He picked up his things from the little alley he'd hidden them in and began walking boldly down the sidewalk of Main Street. There weren't any other pedestrians, and only a car or truck passed occasionally. The town smelled like decay.

Ronnie reached the train yard around two PM. He tried to stay inconspicuous, listening to the men talk. Eventually one spotted him and came over to where he was standing in a shadowed area.

"Plannin' on going somewheres?"

"Yessir, I am. I need to find out which train goes to Helix."

"Got a ticket?" Pause. "Hahaha, just messin' with you, boy. There's one leaving tonight, but you gotta wait until dark. I'll show you a good car to ride. You can just settle in a corner and wait."

Ronnie was relieved. He was tired, and the thought of running alongside a moving train and trying to jump it made his stomach queasy.

"I hope you got a coat. It might be hot now, but that wind blowin' through the open doors can be right chilly."

Ronnie looked down.

"It's all right, boy, I'll find you one. Everybody gotta learn the ropes. Go lay low somewhere until dark, and then look for me. I'll be here. Sho' ain't going nowhere, not for a while."

"Thank you, sir."

"Haha, I ain't no sir, but you're welcome anyway, young gent."

The next few hours were the longest of Ronnie's life. He had to keep moving from place to place to keep from drawing attention to himself, but he never got far from the train yard. Thoughts began to crowd his head, noisy and hard to understand. He had to keep repeating to himself "stay calm, everything's going to be all right." He almost wished that he was home, where at least he knew the reason for the noise and confusion. Almost. He remembered the smoldering ruins of home, and something else his Grandma used to say… "If wishes were horses then beggars would ride." He didn't care, though; he was glad home was gone, and that he was gone. Soon he'd be on his way to Helix, a man. A free man.

Finally, darkness fell. His friend was waiting at the train yard with an old dark coat and a black toboggan. He steered Ronnie to an empty boxcar.

"Just huddle up in the corner there and be invisible, she'll be rolling any time now. And son… be careful. Watch out for the bulls. There'll be one stop before Helix to add on some cars. Just stay put. Second stop, you get off and get out of sight, right?"

Ronnie nodded. "Thanks, Mister."

"Just call me Ham" he replied. "You get in any trouble, just come look me up. We all gotta watch out for each other, right?"

Ronnie nodded again, and crawled into the boxcar.

He slept surprisingly well, even though Ham had been right about the wind. The rumble of the train rocked him to a dreamless sleep, something he was always thankful for. He awoke when it stopped, panicking for a minute that he'd slept through the first stop. After a few minutes, he realized that he couldn't have. He heard men talking in the distance, and felt a jolt as they coupled more empty cars on down the line. He saw some lights shining, like flashlights, but none came near him. It wasn't long before the train lurched forward and began to roll.

Just as he was beginning to relax again, a man jumped into the car with him. Another of his Grandma's sayings came to mind; the man looked like death sucking on a lifesaver. He was dirty, unshaven and rail thin. Ronnie didn't like him immediately, even as he smiled and introduced himself as Shorty. His mouth smiled, but his eyes didn't.

After a little small talk about where they were headed, Shorty moved over beside Ronnie. "Be warmer this way." He reached out and touched Ronnie's face. "What's a purty lil' thing like you doin' travellin' all alone? Bad things can happen, you know… bad things."

Ronnie didn't like the way he was looking at him. He pushed his hand from his face.

Shorty grabbed him by the chin with both hands, boney fingers squeezing his cheeks. "Boy, you're just gonna have to take it like a man. I'm takin' what I want from you, and there ain't nothin' you can do about it." He stood up in front of him and began to unbuckle his belt. "Best be gittin' outta them clothes, boy."

The car was suddenly filled with crows. Ronnie watched as both of his legs kicked forward, saw them kick Shorty in the crotch. He saw the wide-eyed look on Shorty's face as he tumbled out of the door and was pulled beneath the train. He saw it all through the crows, like watching it on TV with a lot of static. Ronnie banged his head against the back of the car until things looked normal again. There. Just like it was, he thought. Just me going to Helix. No bad things. No crows. No scarecrows.

He didn't sleep anymore. For the next hour he rode, thinking, trying not to think. Trying not to think about his Grandma holding him against her soft floppy breasts, calling him her "Little Man." Trying not to think about Jay, and how much he wished he was here with him. Trying not to wonder when he'd really see that field of children with their black balloons. The train began to slow down, and he knew he'd arrived.

Helix looked like hell. Old brick buildings with bars on the windows, others boarded up. Pot-holed streets and cracked sidewalks. Ronnie knew that there was a cotton mill nearby, and a lot of cotton fields. He knew there were more bars than there were churches, too. Jay had told him a lot about the place, but he'd never imagined how run-down it looked. At 4:00 AM, there were only a few stoplights and streetlights to try and pierce the darkness that was Helix. They failed miserably. He spotted the headlights of a car and slipped into the shadows. It was a police car, driving very slowly. Once it passed, he ducked into an alley and lay with his head in a doorway, using the smelly old coat he'd been given as a pillow. "This place smells like death," he thought, as the twinkling little stars gathered around to lull him to sleep.

He awoke with rain in his face. The skies were dark, even though he could tell by the noise that it was morning. He huddled in the doorway and finally allowed himself to cry. Thunder rolled and lightning cracked the sky. He only allowed himself a few minutes of crying. After all, he was a man now. Men didn't cry. They saw a problem, they solved it. His first problem was that he was wet and hungry. The old woman's cans were long gone, but he still had money. He left the towel and water bottle in the doorway and walked out of the alley, holding his coat up to cover his head. He immediately spotted a diner a block down the street. The sign said it was "The Pink Platter." There were people inside eating breakfast, the smell of coffee and cigarette smoke strong. He slid into a booth in the corner and looked at the menu while he waited on the waitress. No one seemed to notice him. When the waitress appeared, she didn't bat an eye as he ordered eggs, bacon and coffee. No friendly banter, just a woman too busy to worry about anything but getting orders out and re-filling coffee cups. When he'd finished his meal, he bought a pack of Camels from the cigarette machine. He sat back down and had another cup of coffee and a cigarette. "Yes," he thought, trying not to cough, "I am a man now."

The rain had stopped and the sun was breaking through the clouds. Just one of those sudden summer downpours, he thought.

As he paid his tab, he asked the cashier where the carnival was.

"About two miles down main at the fairgrounds, almost all the way out of town. Don't know why you'd want to go there, though."

"I'm trying to catch up with my crew" Ronnie answered, "I work there."

The woman looked at him for the first time with an air of disgust and said nothing more. "Damn carnies." she muttered as he left. "Sally, wipe down that booth that boy was sitting in."

Chapter Three: Carnies

It was hot and muggy after the rain, and the hike to the fairgrounds left Ronnie tired and sweaty. He held on to his coat and hat, though; you never knew. When he saw that the chain-link fence was locked, it almost knocked the rest of his breath from him. He slumped down and sat with his back against it. Normally he wouldn't have any trouble scaling the fence, but he was so tired... and thirsty. The thirst was what finally gave him the strength to climb over the fence.

The carnival looked empty and grotesque. A Ferris wheel, a merry-go-round, a tilt-a-whirl. Lots of booths, shuttered. One of those things where you try to make the bell ring with a big hammer. The ground was dirt and straw, mostly dirt. The writing on all of the signs promising fun and food were all faded. It looked like it belonged in Helix. "Maybe that's why they set up shop here and never left." he thought. "They belong here." Now he could add disappointment to his bitch list. He'd imagined how much fun it would be to work at a carnival, all the bright colors and happy people.

A voice broke his reverie. "Hey, kid, we're not open 'til three weekdays." The speaker was a fat tattooed man in an undershirt. He was sitting on a little bench that looked like it might break under his weight at any time. Ronnie realized that he didn't even know what day it was, much less the time.

"I need a job. And some water, if you don't mind."

The man reluctantly stood up, opened one of the booths, and handed him a large paper cup full of water. "I'll have to talk to Bo about hirin' you on. You just might be in luck, though. C.C.'s ate up with the cancer, he probably won't be back. Bo's been handling his share of the work. He might appreciate a little help. He should be comin' in any time now. Hell, here he is now."

Bo was a skinny little man with a five o'clock shadow. Droopy-eyed and going bald, he seemed to have appeared out of nowhere.

"Bo, you need some help? This kid's lookin' for a job."

"I need *help*," he answered, "not some kid to give me more work trainin' him."

"I learn fast, Mister." Ronnie chimed in.

"Hmmm… well, we'll see if you work out. You got your shot, kid."

"Thank you, Mister Bo."

"It's just Bo. Short for Bobo. I'm a clown, the only one here now." He smiled a crooked smile. When Ronnie looked at him, their eyes met and it seemed like they shared some secret. They liked each other. Understood each other somehow.

"You got a place to live?"

"Nossir, I don't."

"Enough with the sirs, huh, kid? There's an extra trailer around back, but you don't want that unless you're really broke. You can have C.C.'s room at the hotel. $2.50 a night. He ain't comin' back, poor bastard. You got money?"

"Yeah, I have a little."

"Good. I'm gonna show you how to make a lot more. Right now I gotta go get ready." He disappeared into an old trailer that Ronnie hadn't even realized was there.

The fat man spoke to him. "You look like shit, son. Go on back to the hotel and get some rest. You can start tomorrow. Bo will come in early and show you what to do. It ain't no big deal." He gave directions to the nearby hotel, instructing him just to grab the key for room 12 off the wall and go on in.

The Pinecomb Hotel looked like hell, but it felt like heaven. A rusty metal framed cot with a pillow and a green army blanket took up most of the small room. There was a bathroom with a sink and a real bathtub. Even though it was stained with who knew what, Ronnie was happy to get a lukewarm bath. The window was already opened, and the air felt good on his body as he climbed into bed. It was just getting dark outside. His stomach growled, and he realized he hadn't eaten since breakfast, but it would have to wait. He sank into a blissful dreamless sleep.

He didn't wake up until ten AM by the clock on the wall. He splashed some water on his face and walked outside. There was an old cinderblock building with bars on the windows adjacent to the hotel.

The neon sign above the door was off, but he could read it... "Shangri-La Bar and Grill." Inside it was dark, with a huge ceiling fan in the center. There were some tables, a jukebox, a cigarette machine, and a long bar. At one end of the bar there were two men in work clothes drinking Schlitz from cans. Ronnie sat at the other end and asked the bartender what they had to eat. The burly man told him that they only had hot dogs, burgers and chips. "Give me two hot dogs, a bag of chips and a coke." While he waited, he noticed a couple of large jars on the bar. He asked about them when the bartender returned with his breakfast... they were pickled eggs and pig's feet. He thought he heard a snicker from the Schlitz men, but he didn't turn to look. He ate as fast as he could and left. He was anxious to get started at the carnival, even though he was a little scared. Things just *had* to work out right. They had to.

"Hey, Killer!" Bo greeted him as he unlocked the gate. Ronnie accepted the nickname without argument, although he wondered why he'd used it. Bo looked exactly as he had the day before, down to the same clothes. "Ready to get started?"

"Damn sure am, Bo."

"There's nothin' to running the games. You just have to make sure people keep playin' 'em. You've been to carnivals before, right? You know how they keep after the marks to get them to play. You just have to be loud and never stop. "Win a prize for your girlfriend!" or "Everybody wins!" shit like that. Whatever comes to mind. You'll see how they do it tonight.

"Bo, I'm not ...uh... *good* with people. You know, talking to strangers and such. How about running the rides? You think I could do that?"

Bo sighed and scratched his chin. "Yeah, I'll show you how to run the Ferris wheel. But there's a lot of other stuff you have to know besides working the levers. A lot of maintenance to keep these old rides going. Some dumbass kid falling off would be bad for business. Just sell the damn corndogs tonight, allright? Think you can do that?"

"Sure, Bo, just show me what to do."

"I'll show you how to run the rides tomorrow. Right now, let me show you all you need to know about corndogs."

"Bo, why have you guys stayed in Helix for so long?" It seemed to Ronnie that it had settled into the town like a disease.

"Lotta reasons, Killer; the people here are stupid enough to keep coming for one thing. Lotta drunks to roll. Besides, this equipment is so old I doubt it would make it to another location. Nobody's asked us to leave. Even the cops are stupid here. All they have for entertainment is a movie house, a bowling alley and a dozen bars. People get drunk and think they can beat the games. They go home broke every time, but they keep coming back and trying again."

The rest of the crew were coming in by then... Salvatore, the fat man from yesterday. An old man no more than four feet high. A fat lady with curly hair and crooked teeth. A couple of pimply kids not much older than Ronnie. A short plump woman with a bowl-cut hairdo and coke bottle glasses. And one young woman with dark red hair and grey eyes. Ronnie thought she was the most beautiful thing he'd ever seen. He asked Bo who she was. "That's Jeannie. She mostly runs the concessions. Too honest for her own good, but she had nowhere else to go."

Ronnie went into the trailer and watched Bo change himself into Bobo. When he was done, he was the god-awfullest, scariest clown he'd ever seen. With a cigarette dangling from his painted lips, he looked like something out of a nightmare. He grinned at Ronnie.

"Suffer the little children to come unto me." Then he laughed. "Don't worry, I'd never hurt a child. But they grow up so fast..."

Chapter Four: Evil Clowns

The first night was scary but exhilarating. It didn't take Ronnie long to run the corndog stand like an old hand. He kept his mouth shut and his ears open. He heard a lot of odd words from the carnies. It was a secret language they used to communicate with each other so the townies couldn't understand them, but he was picking up on some of it. He went back to his room that night feeling satisfied.

The next morning, Bo showed the boy how to run the rides, letting him do it himself after each time. "Nothin' much to this, this is the easiest part. What you want to remember is not to let them ride for too long; just long enough to make them want to pay to ride again. You got a watch?"

Ronnie admitted that he didn't. Bo pulled up his sleeve. There were six watches on his arm. "You can use one of these tonight. It's Friday, so you'll have at least one of your own before the nights over.

That night after the carnival shut down, he went with Bo to an alley near one of the bars. They waited in the darkness for a few minutes in silence. "Just watch," Bo whispered when he heard the door open. A middle-aged man on spindly legs walked by the alley. Bo pulled him in and proceeded to beat the crap out of him. He kept kicking the man as he lay on the ground. Finally he took his wallet and watch.

"Here ya go, Killer." He handed the watch to Ronnie. "This is where you make your real money."

Ronnie wiped the blood from the watch on his pants leg and put it on his wrist.

He found out during the first week that he hated the sounds of screaming kids and carnival music. He also discovered that the work was tedious and boring. What made it worthwhile were the excursions with Bo after work into town, sapping drunks and stealing their money and valuables. That was exciting. He felt alive then. Bo was a good friend, and never tried to cheat him out of his share. Also, the nights he worked the Ferris wheel were not as bad because he could see Jeannie at the concession stands. She always smiled at him, and he always awkwardly turned his eyes away. He wanted to talk to her, but had no

172

idea what to say. One night after work, Ronnie and Bo sat outside looking at the empty night.

Bo took a drag from his cigarette. "You know why I call you Killer?"

"No, I don't."

"It's in your eyes. You got the killer instinct. You ever done a murder before?"

Ronnie looked at his shoes. "None that I didn't have to."

"Well, it can be *fun*, you know. Everybody's gotta die sometime. You deciding when makes you kinda like God."

"I guess."

"I strangled a woman when I was about your age. Just put my hands around her throat and squeezed the life out of her. It was really somethin' to see the life leave her body."

Ronnie couldn't help but be fascinated by his story. "No, I never done nothin' like that. I was always kinda... out of myself... like I was watching somebody else do it."

"Do it for yourself one time and you'll be hooked on it. Hard to stop killin' once you've done it that way. There's a man lives a couple miles from here, a stingy old bastard. Keeps all his money in the house. He's got dogs, though. I'll take care of the dogs, you take care of him."

Ronnie thought about it for a minute. "OK. I don't like the idea of killin' dogs, though, they're just doin' their job."

"And we're just doin' ours. We'll do it next Wednesday, when we can get out of here a little early. You kinda sweet on that Jeannie girl, aren't you?"

"Yeah, I guess I am."

"Talk to her tomorrow. She won't bite you." He rose, stretched, and yawned. "Let's call it a night."

"But what do I say to her?"

"Just say "Hello, they call me Killer.""

Ronnie lay in his cot for a long time that night, staring at the ceiling. He'd be thirteen soon, and his body had sprouted hair in unwanted places. He didn't think much about the planned killing, that was just business. His thoughts kept returning to Jeannie. She made him feel like he'd never felt before. He couldn't get a handle on it. It bothered him that he couldn't. He imagined scenarios where he'd try to talk to her and she'd laugh at him, or slap him, or ignore him. But then, he'd imagine her smiling at him, kissing him, laughing with him about some stupid thing. He wondered what she felt like. He wanted to know.

The next afternoon he took Bo's suggestion. He walked right up to Jeannie and said "Hi. My name's Ronnie, but they call me Killer."

"Pleased to meet you, I'm Jeannie. Why do they call you Killer? Are you a lady-killer?"

"No, it's just something Bo made up to call me, probably 'cause he couldn't remember my name."

She smiled at him, and he didn't know whether to jump for joy or run like hell. He stood there in silence for a moment before looking at her again. "Pleased to meet you too, Jeannie." The name sounded delicious on his lips. "I'll see you around."

His heart was thumping as he went to check the rides to make sure there weren't any loose bolts. There usually were. He'd done it. He'd talked to her, and she to him, and she wasn't disgusted. The world wasn't as ugly as it had been five minutes ago. Taking out a pack of Camels rolled up in his tee-shirt sleeve, he lit one.

Suddenly Bo was standing right beside him, in full clown dress. "Just don't let that gal make you go soft on me, boy. Remember tonight."

"Jesus Christ, you scare me the way you pop up outta nowhere like that! Don't worry, I'm ready for tonight." He wished that he was talking about taking Jeannie out to a movie or something, though. She had softened him up a bit, somehow.

The night went badly. Even though Bo was an excellent shot, the night was starless and the dogs appeared out of nowhere. He was bitten twice before the last yelp. Inside, Ronnie looked at the helpless old man as Bo ransacked the house. He had no stomach for killing him. He couldn't even fight back.

"He's seen us. Do it!" Bo's blood was all over the house.

Ronnie wrapped his hands around the trembling old man's neck and pressed his thumbs down. He could hear crows in the distance, but this was in the here and now. He could feel the life force creeping out of the old man as his face turned red, then purple.

"I found the money! You through in there?"

"Yeah, I'm through." Ronnie released his grip and the old man fell to the floor. Dead weight, now.

"Killer, we're rich! There must be a thousand dollars each here!"

Ronnie wasn't all that happy about the money, or the murder. He didn't say anything to Bo about it, but he thought how he was feeling just as trapped here now as he'd been at his parents' house.

"So how did it feel? Was it like I told you?"

"Yeah, Bo, just like you said."

Chapter Five: Jeannie

Ronnie knew that a carnie throwing money around would draw the suspicion of even the Helix police. He buried most of his share in a cigar box, in a place only he knew about. It felt good to know it was there if he needed it, though, and he didn't have to worry about paying the rent. As it was, the cops were out at the fairgrounds asking questions several times. The crimes had been in the next county, but close enough to throw suspicion on the despised carnies. His sudden sullenness made Jeannie more intrigued with him; she talked to him more, attempting to draw him out. Ronnie felt dead inside. He thought sometimes of running away with Jeannie, maybe to the beach, but he knew that he couldn't run from himself. He *was* a killer, now. He asked her to run away with him one night when he'd been drinking. She laughed, and he laughed too, like it was a joke. But he was thinking to himself that life was one big joke, and he was the butt of it.

Bo had bought an almost-new car, a '54 Buick Special. They began riding as far away as they could during the day, just looking for an easy mark. Then they'd come back late at night and do the crime. It was a lot of riding time, but things were too hot in Helix after the murder to even roll drunks. Bo was increasingly violent and erratic. He began wearing his clown gear all of the time. One night Ronnie watched him rape a woman in his clown costume. He didn't kill her; he said he wanted to give her nightmares for the rest of her life. He was beginning to give Ronnie nightmares. He felt that things were closing in on him, and there was nothing he could do about it. He felt that there was always a crow following him, just over his shoulder.

Even though there was little time for frivolous things, he and Jeannie managed to talk more and more. He found out that she was sixteen (the same age he'd been lying about being from the beginning) and that she'd run away from a bad home life at fourteen. They had a lot in common, but there were glaring differences. She was sweet and outgoing, with curly dark almost-red hair and light grey eyes. He was introverted and dark eyed, but the long sandy hair combed back and the muscles he'd developed did make him look closer to sixteen than thirteen. One night he blew off Bo and she came up to his room. They made love awkwardly. It was both of their first times, but it sealed their relationship. They were now officially in love. Love. He'd never really known such a thing existed. Ronnie wondered if he dared to let himself believe that there really were good things in the world. He wished that he could take her out, go to the movies or just cruising, but there wasn't much time or even a way to accomplish those things. They had to be satisfied with her visits to him several nights a week after work. Soon she was sleeping with him every night. He stopped going out with Bo after work, anxious to get home to Jeannie.

Bo said that he understood, and that they should probably let things cool down a little anyway. They'd been driving farther and farther out to do their crimes, but it was surely becoming obvious to the cops that Helix, if not the carnival itself, was the hub of all of this criminal activity. Besides, they had money. They'd been doing things just for the hell of it lately. It was Bo's idea of fun.

The days tripped over each other. Soon a year had passed. It seemed like ten to Ronnie. Working at the carnival, occasional outings with Bo, seeing Jeannie. He began drinking more; it helped with the dreams. The accusatory faces, the blood, the horrible things that he'd done and saw that came back to haunt him at night. Bo never had a problem with bad dreams, he'd told him so. Ronnie realized that he himself was fucked up, but Bo was a stone cold psychopath. It was getting time for them to part ways. He didn't like the way Bo had been looking at Jeannie, for one thing, but he'd had enough senseless violence. He wanted to go somewhere cool and quiet and peaceful. Maybe even marry Jeannie. But no kids. He swore to himself that he'd never bring a child into this fucked-up world.

Ronnie wasn't a child any longer; he was an almost-fifteen year old man. He knew the implications when Jeannie told him one night that she was "late."

"You can't have it. We have to find a doctor."

"You want to kill your own child?"

"You know how I feel about having children. Can you honestly say you want to bring a child into this world?"

"I don't want to kill it."

"It's not a baby yet. It's a speck that can be removed. You're not thinking clearly. Can you imagine trying to raise a baby living this life we live?"

"Maybe we can get away. Have a real home. Send him to school, be good parents."

"You're fucking dreaming!" he slammed the door and walked out into the cool night air.

Ronnie walked down to the fairgrounds and sat on the old familiar bench, chain smoking. Loretta the coke-bottle-glasses lady and Salvatore came and sat down with him.

"Problems at home?"

"No. No problems." Then to Loretta "You ever had any kids?"

"Two, a boy and a girl."

"Ever get rid of one?"

"What do you mean? Abortion?"

"Yeah."

"Yes." She said, very quietly.

"I need to find a doctor… for Jeannie."

Loretta walked to her trailer and came back a few minutes later holding a scrap of paper. "This is his name and address, if he's still there."

Salvatore shook his head and walked away. Loretta sat there beside Ronnie for a while.

"It'll be allright."

Ronnie shook his head from side to side, looking down at his feet. "Nothing's ever allright, Loretta. Never."

The next two weeks were a blur of working, drinking, getting into fights, and arguing with Jeannie. Then one day he forgot to do a maintenance check on the tilt-a-whirl. One of the cars spun off and injured a young mother and her child. They weren't seriously hurt, but the carnival was shut down for three days while it was investigated. Salvatore told him that he was sorry, but he'd have to go. Jeannie finally won the argument, not just because he'd lost his job, but with the words "If you make me do this, I'll never love you again the way I did before."

"We have to leave, then. I'll get a job, maybe in a factory somewhere, somewhere nice. But we need money. We need a car. I've gotta go talk to Bo."

He found Bo at the Shangri-La, sitting at the bar in full clown gear drinking Ancient Age. He was either drunk or just crazy, you could never tell with him.

"Bo, I need to make some money, fast."

"Well hello, stranger. Come back when you need somethin' from me, huh? No fuckin' dice. I'll give you twenty dollars to fuck Jeannie, though."

Ronnie drew back his arm to hit him, but he caught his wrist.

"Don't fuck with me, Killer. You know what I can do."

People were staring, so Ronnie backed down. "Go to hell!"

"You first."

Chapter Six: The Road to Freedom

It happened in October, around 3:00AM. He dreamed he was twelve again, in his driveway at home playing with his army men. His mother came out holding a cupcake with a candle in it and told him that it was his birthday. He couldn't blow out the candle, though; the flame kept getting higher and higher. Suddenly there were clowns dancing all around him, all of them dead-eyed with black crow wings. Then Bo was shaking him, shouting at him:

"What have you done?! What the fuck have you done?!!"

He was standing at the fairgrounds, still holding a gas can in his hand. Everything was going up in flames. He hit Bo in the head with the gas can, knocking him to the ground. Pulling a straight razor from his shoe, he slit his throat. Just like that, without a thought. Bo made a gurgling sound as he tried to speak, tried to comprehend what had just happened. Ronnie leaned down close to him and whispered. "No, *you* first. See you in hell, you soulless motherfucker."

Ronnie took Bo's car and sped back to the hotel, pounding on the door. He didn't know where his key was.

"Wake up! Jeannie! Wake up, we gotta go!"

She appeared at the door in a nightgown, looking confused and terrified at once.

"Get your clothes and LET'S GO!" He opened the closet and began throwing things on the bed.

She stuffed some clothes in a bag and followed him to the car, barefoot and in her nightgown. She knew this wasn't the time to ask questions. She could see the fire over at the carnival, turning the night sky red as they sped away.

"Goddamnit, the money! I have to get the money!"

He pulled the car over to the side of the road and told her to wait there for him. Scrambling through the woods in the darkness, he looked for the marks he'd left so that he could find the place he'd buried the cigar box. At last he found it and dug it up with his hands. Pulling the decaying box up, he ran back to the car.

When he returned, Jeannie had dressed in jeans and a tee-shirt. Ronnie pulled her close to him. "We're on the road to freedom now, baby!"

180

(From The Helix Review: The C&C Carnival was burned to the ground last night. Although there were no injuries from the fire, Boyd Hendricks, 36, was found murdered at the site. His car and two carnival workers are missing, and are wanted for questioning by the Helix police. The workers are Jeannie Griffin, 17, and a male of unknown age known only as Ronnie, alias Killer. If you have any information regarding this matter, please contact the Helix police department.)

Charles Goodwin was an investigator for the Helix police department. A meticulous man, he was well-suited to the job. He'd been working with detectives from the three surrounding counties for months now. He was convinced that most of the serious crime that had begun almost a year ago was the work of the same criminal, or criminals. He'd been zeroing in on Bo and Ronnie when the fire broke out and Ronnie disappeared. "I'll get you, you son-of-a-bitch", he thought angrily. "You can run, but you can't hide from me. I *will* get you."

Charles came home late gain and poured himself a Scotch. He ignored Julia when she told him that his dinner was cold, and the kids were already in bed. He'd been ignoring her a lot, lately, he knew. But once this case was settled, once he had the bastard behind bars, everything would be different. He noticed a drawing taped to the refrigerator. Stick figures of a mom and two kids holding balloons. There was no dad in the picture.

When he came home the next evening, his wife had taken their children and moved in with her mother. He was almost relieved. There'd be no distractions from his single-minded purpose now. Find out who this killer was and arrest him. He began making phone calls.

Chapter Seven: The Road to Hell

July 29th, 1954

Jay was driving a tanker truck for Texaco when the news reached him that his parents were dead and his old house burned. He'd just returned from a long haul, looking forward to a couple of days off. When he reached his small apartment, there was a card stuck in the screen door. "It is with great regret that we must inform you…" He stood there and read it twice before it sunk in. His dad, he could give a rat's ass. But his mom. And where was Ronnie? They'd only found the remains of *two* bodies. "Goddamnit, Ronnie!"

He went inside and got a beer from the refrigerator. He sat down and drank deeply, staring straight ahead. That one thought kept pounding in his head. "Goddamnit, Ronnie! Goddamnit!" Where could he have gone? Where would he go?

Jay had been doing pretty well the last couple of years. He did his job, kept his nose clean, and managed not to let his quick temper get the best of him. Now he wished like hell that he'd sent for Ronnie. He'd been selfish, he thought; he could have brought him up here to Rockford and kept him out of trouble. The truth was, he'd wanted to forget everything about his home life. He hadn't had any contact with them at all for over two years. Ronnie had been what, nine or ten the last time he saw him? "Goddamnit, Ronnie, what the hell did you do?" He threw his empty beer bottle at the wall.

He awoke with empty Pabst bottles all around and full ashtrays. His head felt like hammers were pounding it inside. Jay wasn't usually a big drinker. He made some coffee and tried to sort things out in his mind. What should he do? What could he do? He swallowed some aspirin with his coffee. It tasted like regret, bitter and vile.

He called his boss and told him that he needed some time off. He had a week's paid vacation coming, he could take two. After that, they needed him back. What could he say but okay? He'd have to worry about the job if the time came. Right now, he had to find Ronnie. Packing a suitcase, he remembered the one thing that Ronnie had always listened to with rapt attention; when he talked about the carnival. "Okay," he thought, "at least I know where I'm headed. Helix."

It was a long drive from Illinois to North Carolina. Jay's '51 Chevy was reliable, but untested on a long road trip. He filled some containers with water in case it overheated, which was very likely. Stopping to withdraw most of his money from the bank and gas up, he hit the road.

Just as quickly, he pulled over and took a map out of the glove compartment. He realized how long and twisted his route from Helix to Rockford had been. He'd ended up in Rockford via Jacksonville Florida, Fort Worth Texas, Sacramento California, and finally Aberdeen Washington, back when he was riding the rails. He needed to find the quickest route straight to Helix. The lines on the map seemed to move as he remembered the places he'd been and the people he'd met. Especially *her*. The one he'd left behind in Aberdeen, promising to return. He never did. Life got in the way. Driving a truck satisfied his travelling bone. That was the only way he'd been able to stay in one place for two years. Finally he shook off his reverie and headed for State Street, where he'd pick up Highway 51. "The road to hell is paved with good intentions." Why did he think that as he left?

Jay felt mixed emotions as he drove. He had his life in order, finally; what was he doing risking everything this way? But Ronnie had always looked up to him, almost like a hero. He remembered more than once taking a beating meant for Ronnie, of sitting on the porch with him telling him stories. It was his fault that the little fuck had run off to the carnival. He had to do something. But how would he take care of him? He wasn't even at home most of the time. Put him in an orphanage? Hell, no, he wouldn't do that. What was he going to do once he reached Helix?

Suddenly there was a deer in the headlights, just standing there staring at him. He swerved to miss it and ran the Chevy into a ditch. With a broken left arm and several cracked ribs, it would be months before he could think about going back. He lay in a hospital bed, miserable physically and mentally. He blamed himself, he blamed Ronnie, he blamed God, but nothing could change the situation now.

He received his draft notice while still recovering. It was deferred, but he'd have to go once he was healed. The army had plenty of other jobs besides being a foot soldier. Even walking with a limp couldn't keep him from driving for Uncle Sam.

It would be years before he could try to find Ronnie. All he could do now was to hope for the best. He tried to remember how to pray.

Chapter Eight: At Large

Ronnie's exuberance subsided as they drove. He was driving a murdered man's stolen car with a pregnant girlfriend, and had no idea where he was going. They stayed in cheap hotels, trying to keep the car hidden as well as possible. They always bought a newspaper and scanned the 'Help Wanted' section, but all he knew was carnival work. They actually came upon a carnival in some small town, but when he asked about a job all he got was wide eyes and shaking heads. The word had been passed from Helix about him. They knew who he was. Every carnie in the country had probably heard. News like that spreads fast.

Finally, he realized that they'd been travelling in a more or less westward direction.

"California! Jeannie, California! All along the coast there they have amusement parks. We'll live near the beach, I'll work, and you can stay home and raise our baby right!"

Jeannie brightened. It seemed like a good plan. Ronnie slept that night for the first time since they'd left without dreaming of clowns and crows.

The next few years passed by without incident. First they pushed Bo's car into the Pacific. Then Ronnie got a job at the newly constructed Disneyland. They were married and had a son, Eric. Things went well for the young couple. Ronnie's harsh past seemed to be just that... the past. A small house, a car, they were living the American dream. In November of 1962, he was even finally reunited with Jay, who had done his time in the army and tracked him down. He spent a week on their couch catching up. Neither of them brought up the fires at home or the carnival. Jay didn't see any point in it now, Ronnie had turned out okay. There were things that Jay had done in the army that he didn't want to talk about, either. They both still had occasional nightmares, but they didn't talk about it. For all their talking, there was actually quite a bit omitted.

Neither knew that Charles Goodwin existed, but he knew about them. He was looking for Jay as well now, thinking... hoping... that he'd find Ronnie with him. Phone calls were made and letters sent to anywhere he thought either of them might be. He had no photographs, but he had descriptions. He also believed now that Ronnie was responsible for two fires and at least three deaths.

His break came when a former carnie who was also working at Disneyland called the local police department and told them that he thought they might want this guy that he worked with. He'd seen a sketch of him in the post office. They called Goodwin.

Two days after Jay left, there was a knock on the door. Two cops were standing on the porch.

"Are you Ronnie Baxter? We have a warrant for your arrest."

They led a shocked Ronnie to the car in handcuffs. Jeannie was crying, Eric was crying, and his head was filled with his old black-winged friends. He'd never forget the date, November 10th, 1962. It was the last time he'd ever see Jeannie and Eric.

Goodwin had been working for years on his case. Sometimes he had to put it away for a while for more current crimes, other times there was just no new information to be had. But he had bulldogged it, and finally found out who Ronnie was, and now at last, where he was. It didn't give him the satisfaction he'd thought it would as he walked into the door of his empty house. It would give him even less when he heard the verdict.

Returned to North Carolina for trial, he was sentenced to five years for the carnival arson. They couldn't convict him of murder, there wasn't enough evidence. It had been too long; there were never any witnesses, and a lot of evidence had disappeared over the years. Charles left the courtroom and put his fist through the mirror at home. He didn't like what he saw there anymore.

Suddenly everything was gone. Ronnie served his time at Caswell Correctional Center in North Carolina. Jeannie tried to visit several times that first year, but Ronnie wouldn't see her. He didn't want her or his son to see him in this terrible place.

There were no problems with the other inmates; they quickly learned to fear him. Inside, he was called "Crazy-Eyes". He even developed a little cult following who wanted to stay in his good graces for protection. Paul Chandler was the only one inside to get close to him. Paul was in for minor theft, but they took a liking to each other rightaway. Paul was cool in all situations, and became Ronnie's right-hand man.

Prison life was more years of monotony. He hated the routine, the knowledge that he couldn't go anywhere further than the exercise yard. Being locked up was the worst thing that could have happened to him. The good memories of the last few years quickly blurred, and the old memories came back to haunt. The crows were always there in his head. Somehow he managed to get a year taken off of his sentence for "good behavior". He walked out on April 30th, 1966. He didn't even go home to see if Jeannie had waited for him. He figured she was with Jay. In his mind, it was Jay who had turned him in, jealous of his family. He probably swooped right in like a crow and took them away. Ronnie was different now, different than he'd ever been. He was gone down the road…

He broke parole two hours after walking out of the gate. With five dollars in his pocket, he began hopping trains, headed for San Francisco. He knew how to get money. He knew how to survive.

The world had changed a lot in four years. The United States was a bubbling cauldron, ready to boil over. He learned quickly what was happening, and knew that his instincts had been right. 'Frisco was the place to be. That was where the flower children with their black balloons waited. He wouldn't work for anyone ever again. He'd have people working for him. Standing on the brink of the Summer of Love, he was conjuring the Summer of Death. Fuck the world.

In San Francisco, he made money the old-fashioned way; rolling drunks, muggings, a little B&E. He had let his hair grow out, for no other reason than that he just didn't care anymore. With that and his Salvation Army clothes, business owners mistook him for a hippie, and showed their contempt. He showed his contempt back, in a much more violent manner. The hippies on the street embraced him as one of their own. He felt closer to them than he had ever felt towards his own family. They were a lot like the carnies. He never hurt them, but the businessmen caught hell.

Two things happened in May of '67; he heard The Doors' 'The End' and dropped acid for the first time. He declared himself God, and a lot of people believed him. The core of these were twelve people he dubbed "The Lost Children." Jack, one of the six men, had a rich father. He rented a large house in the Bay area where they held big parties with some of the new bands that were springing up out of nowhere. Vicki, a dark-eyed Gypsy girl, became his "wife". She said that when she looked into his eyes she could see a lost soul, mourning its very existence. He told her not to look too long; she might see other things that she wouldn't like.

Paul from Caswell was the happy thief in the group, and became Ronnie's right-hand man once again. He'd been released just a week after Ronnie and headed straight for 'Frisco. His excuse for his thievery was that he was "sticking it to the man", but the truth was that he was addicted to the thrill of it. The summer fell around their shoulders like a noisy, colorful party. The balloons were not the black ones Ronnie had expected, but psychedelic, multi-colored ones which bounced around instead of rising up. Still, he knew better than to embrace hope. Hope had died. All he could do was follow the path to its end. By the end of the summer, people were holding funerals for it, declaring 'The Summer of Love' dead. It came as no surprise to Ronnie.

Ronnie's "Family" grew closer over the next few months. There were still parties and music, but he had begun dressing all in black. His favorite song was The Crazy World of Arthur Brown's "Fire". The Vietnam protests were serious business now. The entire world reminded him of his childhood life in the little green-shingled house. He wanted to burn it all. He wanted those black balloons to rise, and him with them. *He* was the God of Hellfire. Instructions on how to make homemade bombs were as easy to come by as acid. They began bombing upscale restaurants and businesses, always leaving graffiti with the words "Kill the pigs" or "Die, pigs." Even the members of The Lost Children closest to him thought that they were doing it as a protest. Only he knew that it was his intention to set the world on fire. The first time he heard the slogan "Burn, Baby, Burn" he actually cracked a rare smile. There were others out there now, following his lead. They were going to burn this motherfucker to the ground.

In August of '69, Charles Manson and his family went on a rampage of murder that infuriated Ronnie. These amateurs were going to fuck up his big plans that had been slowly moving forward. Abbie Hoffman and his group had been a good distraction from his own, but Manson's family's antics were going to fuck up everything. Everyone with long hair or a beard was a suspected murderer now. Jack's dad stopped paying the rent on the house when he discovered that Jack hadn't been back to school since the fall of '68. They needed a lot of money, and they needed it fast. Where was all the money? In the banks, of course.

Ronnie took Paul and his other most trusted member besides Vicky, a tall afroed man known as Mingo. They wore Marilyn Monroe masks and carried AK-47s, and came into the First National Bank on the Boulevard firing. The tellers handed over all the money in the registers, but said that they couldn't open the safe. There was no time to argue, they had to get in and out. The police would be there any minute. Seven customers were wounded; two would die later.

The take was unsatisfactory, although it solved their problems for the present. It had been exhilarating, though, for them all. They quickly came up with the idea of bringing a bomb next time to blow the safe. Ronnie would have to do some research on what size he would need, but it seemed doable. The problem was, all these little side projects were interfering with his master plan. He wanted war in the streets of America. He wanted to burn it all to the ground, start anew. But the cogs were turning much more slowly than he wanted. The crows were cawing louder again. He could feel things slipping away.

Chapter Nine: Black Balloons

Dec 17th, 1969

Jeannie was fairly happy with Jay. He'd come in to help while Ronnie was in prison, and things just happened. Neither of them meant for it to happen, it just did. Eric seemed happy enough, and that was the main thing as far as she was concerned. Jay did have a quick temper, but he had a kind heart. He'd never raised a hand to her or Eric. When she found out that Ronnie had been released, she was only mildly surprised that he hadn't come home. Maybe he had, and seen Jay's car in the drive. It was over with Ronnie, anyway. That was another life, and it seemed so long ago. Still, she thought of him often, wondered how he was doing. What he was doing.

One night she was half-watching the CBS Evening News when she saw him. She almost didn't recognize him with his shoulder-length unkempt hair and a beard, but she knew those eyes. But this wasn't him, not *her* Ronnie. This was a madman, talking crazy talk about fighting a war in the streets of America. It was just a little news clip, with Walter Cronkite adding that he was wanted for parole violation and as a suspect in several other crimes. He was thought to be in San Francisco. They showed his old mug shot from when he'd been arrested. This wasn't the same man. Not anymore.

Charles Goodwin was watching the news that night too. He called the police department in San Francisco and told them everything he knew about him. They were polite, but seemed to think it old and useless information. Irrelevant. He'd spent years on this case, *years*! he thought. He'd lost his family, lost everything trying to get and keep this killer locked up. They hadn't listened to him at the parole hearing. Now these big-time cops didn't even want his help. Charles threw his badge in the trash, pulled out his service revolver and stuck it in his mouth. There was no one there to hear the shot.

Ronnie and The Lost Children had collected an arsenal. They had failed in their mission. There was a siege mentality now, holed up in the beach house. Ronnie gave a little speech, freeing anyone who wanted to leave to do so. No one did.

"This is the end, beautiful friends, the end… we're fighting a war that we can't win. But we can go out with a bang. A big one."

189

They cheered.

When Jeannie told Jay what she'd seen on TV, he told her to sit tight and take care of Eric. He was going to San Francisco. There were tears in his eyes. As he got into the car, Scott Mackenzie was singing "If you're going to San Francisco." He turned it off, and cried as he drove.

He called the police there and told them who he was. He was just in time. A small army of police were gathering outside the house. He begged them for an opportunity to talk to Ronnie. Like a scene from an old TV show, they used the bullhorn to ask if he could come in. After a long minute, the door opened a crack and someone yelled for him to come. Once inside, the door slammed behind him.

Jay hadn't seen weaponry like this since the army. Goddamn, these people had grenades! Ronnie was sitting coolly in a lounge chair, as if this were some Sunday visit. Except for the revolver in his hand. The others were at the windows with their automatic rifles.

"Hello, brother. Nice of you to drop in."

"Ronnie, what the hell are you doing? You're going to get yourself and all of these people killed. For what? For nothing."

"Everything dies, Brother. How are Jeannie and Eric?"

"They're fine. You knew that I'd take care of them. Now why don't you do the right thing for once?"

"I did the right thing once. You took my family away, and now you want me to listen to you? I should shoot you right now."

"I didn't take them away, you abandoned them. What was I supposed to do?"

"You set me up. You called the cops on me and had me taken away from them because you were jealous, you son-of-a-bitch."

"That's not what happened. It was that detective from Helix. He finally found you. All I could do was to try and protect them while you were gone."

"You're a lying motherfucker!" Ronnie stood up and walked towards Jay, pointing the gun. "I want to be close enough to see your eyes when I kill you."

190

When he was close enough, Jay's army training kicked in, the disarmament procedure. They struggled for the gun. The room was filled with crows, visible only to Ronnie. They were everywhere, he couldn't see for the damned things. Time slowed down to a crawl. The gun went off, and Ronnie slowly slipped to the floor. There was a strange look of relief on his careworn face. Suddenly there were children in white in a field, holding black balloons. One of the balloons had Ronnie's name on it. He took it and began drifting skyward with it. Looking down, he saw the children waving goodbye to him. He smiled at them and kept drifting upwards. There was a bright star in the sky, and that was where he was going.

At the sound of the shot, the edgy policemen began firing. Time sped up again to a chaotic pace. The Family fired back. Jay dove behind a sofa. The house was shattered with gunfire, blood spattered everywhere. It didn't last five minutes. Everyone in the house but Jay was dead. Ronnie hadn't lived to see them go out without quite a big of a bang as he'd imagined. He was floating towards the bright star holding his black balloon.

...

(From The San Francisco Chronicle: December 21st, 1969: Thirteen people were killed by police last night at a house in the Bay area, seven males and six females. Ronnie Baxter and his "family" of militants were hiding out in the house, heavily armed. They were wanted for several bombings and at least two bank robberies. Baxter's brother, who had gone into the house to try to talk him down, survived. No police officers were harmed.)

...

Southern Gothic

Somewhere deep in South Carolina, there is a house made of wood with peeling white paint. The windows are all shaded with old yellowed shades, and the floors inside are aged yellow linoleum and hardwood. Tall brush, weeds and trees almost hide it from the world. Out in the backyard is a huge tangle of rusting junk; old cars, refrigerators, coils of wire; a plethora of ungainly brown objects with weeds growing up between. This is where we lived, in another time. We were a family of five, Mad Rosa's family. The nights were heavy and dripped sweat. Rosa's room in the attic was the hottest. If she hadn't already been insane, it would surely have driven her to madness.

Our father was Edsel, a quiet cigar-smoking man who didn't believe in throwing anything away. Our mother was Lucinda, a woman who seemed to think that smiling would cause wrinkles, and rarely did. Rosa was the oldest child. She'd been locked in the attic for as long as my elder sister Joan and I could remember. I was the youngest. My name was Amos. I speak in the past tense because we're all dead now.

There was an old graveyard next to the house; mainly tombstones, a couple of stone mausoleums. The one mausoleum that made this cemetery stand out was a brick one with a glass window. Inside was a saddle and bridle, photographs of the occupant, and other things that he'd loved in life. His mother had gone a little crazy when he died so young, and had this built for him. When I was young, there would always be fresh flowers outside of it, though I never met the woman who left them.

Anyway, from what I've gathered over the years, Rosa began seeing this boy when she was around nine years old. She began hanging around the mausoleum, talking to him. She swore she could see and hear the boy. Back then, there were no doctors to cure the mind, and it was considered a shame to have a mad person in your family. God had brought down his wrath on such a family for some reason, it was thought. So to keep Rosa from wandering in the graveyard talking to spirits, she was locked in the attic. Dad made a little door where they could send up food and take out her waste. Otherwise it stayed locked.

The years went by. My dad passed away first, at the age of fifty-three. My mom followed him shortly thereafter. Joan and I stayed in the house, never marrying. We never thought of letting Rosa out. It was just the way things were. Joan tended the little garden, and I hunted and fished; we went into town only on rare occasions. We didn't like it when we had to. People always seemed to be staring and whispering behind our backs. We were strangers in our own land.

Having no one else, Joan and I began living as man and wife. We had a baby girl when we were in our early twenties. It was a born with a caul, and died shortly after its birth. After that Joan was barren, and we figured that it was for the best. Although I had educated myself well from all the old books in the library, we couldn't send a child to school. People would talk.

Rosa died sometime in August, when I was thirty-seven. We noticed that she wasn't taking her food, and in a day or two the whole house had the stench of death. We discussed giving her a proper burial, but neither of us wanted to go into the attic. It had been closed so long, it somehow seemed wrong to do it. Eventually the smell went away, and we continued on.

One evening when I was coming back from hunting, I saw them. A boy, maybe fifteen, wearing a cowboy hat, and a woman of about forty. Her hair was dark and matted; pale skinned, she had dark circles under her eyes. Both were transparent, and glowed as if filled with moonlight. They were walking from the house toward the graveyard. They didn't seem to notice me. I didn't tell anyone, not even Joan. I didn't want to be locked in the attic the rest of my life. But anytime I was out around twilight, I'd see them, walking to or from the house and the graveyard.

Joan and I grew old in that house. The older I got, the more ghosts I saw. The graveyard was full of them. I still kept my silence. One day a man came and nailed a sign to our door. "Condemned," it said. But no one ever came to tear it down. The house and its occupants seemed to have been forgotten by the world.

Finally, when the ghosts began to enter the house and speak to me, I had to ask Joan.

"Did you see that?"

"Amos, I've been seeing them for years."

"I think they're telling us it's our time."

Joan nodded solemnly.

"Yes, it's time."

We drank the brown bottles of arsenic we'd put away many years ago for this occasion, and sat down on the old sofa to die. It was good to see Rosa again, and our parents. We're all happy now. So many new friends, so much that we lacked when we were alive. Maybe this is really living, and what we called living was death. Just maybe.

Love

Oysterboy and Starfishgirl scramble down the slope from the pink hotel, down to the white dazzle of sand on the beach. Reaching the bottom, they fall into each other's' arms, laughing. At the same instant, they both realize; this is the perfect moment, a bright page in their book of memories that will never fade.

...

Old and dying, Oysterboy takes her wrinkled hand. "Remember that day?" he whispers. She smiles. "It's been a good life, Oysterboy. I love you." And once again, they think the same thought: "I know what heaven is like." "I'll be with you again soon." she says. And he knows she will.